THE UNFORESEEN

by

E. T. Jahn

Published by **Mandrill** a division of Trident Media Company
801 N Pitt Street, Suite 123
Alexandria, VA 22314 USA

www.edenplaza.com

Dedication

To my wife and children for their
advice and encouragement
and to my grandchildren
for brightening my life

-Prologue-

Tom Jenson had come to Nalowale, one of the many remote islands that dotted the great Hawaiian Archipelago, two years ago on January 10, 2003. Ahi Island, a desolate volcanic rock, was his closest neighbor. During the evening he would sit on the lanai of his old Victorian house and sip his after-dinner coffee. He enjoyed watching the western sky turn from bright orange to a soft lavender as the sun sank into the Pacific Ocean. He would listen to the soft breeze rustle the branches of the large palms and inhale the perfumed fragrance of the bougainvillea. Four hundred feet down the mountain was a small village where he went to pick up supplies and an occasional piece of mail from the mainland. The only sound that would break the stillness was the drone of aircraft engines making routine flights over Ahi Island.

On November 1,2005, a reconnaissance aircraft reported seeing activity in and around the dark crater, heralding that Ahi Island, dormant for a hundred years, was soon to awaken from its long sleep. A week later seismographs registered strong tremors, followed by a major earthquake that shook the barren island. Then a disquieting stillness fell over the area.

Two months later, fissures began to open in the crust of the island and flaming lava erupted in a spectacular stream of fire along the crack. Fountains of brilliantly colored lava shot hundreds of feet into the sky like giant arteries pumping out the blood of the earth. For forty days the lava bubbled and spewed hot ash and acrid smoke filled the air with the pungent odor of sulfur.

The island was remote, but planes and boats crowded with tourists from the mainland came out to Ahi, now engulfed in fire and sulfurous gases, to witness the pure wrath of nature.

The now active volcano seethed until, with a great roar, the lava broke through and overflowed the crater with the violence of an exploding sun. Huge amounts of hot rock and pumice were tossed several miles from the crater, and as the molten lava flowed down into the sea, great columns of steam rose several thousand feet into the atmosphere. Those who had witnessed it likened the power and force of it to one of biblical proportions.

The intoxicating fragrance of the balmy Pacific air was suddenly filled with the acrid smell of hot sulfur as thick black smoke began to drift out over the water. The sky over the nearby island of Nalowale was plunged into darkness when black ash filled the air for an entire day. Then it was over, the black smoke dissipated, and the volcano once again slept. Slowly the tour boats pulled away and flights were rescheduled to more traditional sights.

-One-

At the Kaolani Center for Volcanic Research on Oahu Dr. Richard Fleming noted that two months had passed since the last tremor on Ahi. A stocky gray-haired man in his late sixties, had a seriousness that was in stark contrast to the loud island shirts and sandals he favored. The Kaolani Center was funded in part by private donations. The backers of the center considered Fleming one of their most valuable assets.

From his office Dr.Fleming had carefully monitored the progress of the volcano from the first glimmers of flame to the final violent upheaval. He had made several observational flights over the crater and had waited with trepidation for two months after the eruption. Now it looked as though it was all over. Ahi had come to life for a while and then became silent. That was the way with all volcanoes, and Ahi had behaved like any volcano.

He looked again at the file on his desk and examined the material as he had done frequently in the last few months. Some of the reports were yellowed, dating back to the 1960s at the time the center was established. Then there were the more recent ones along with the aerial photographs of the barren island. But there was little covering the years in between. In fact, until all this began in April, he had not even thought about Ahi in thirty years.

Well, it was over now, and all his concern had been for nothing. It was time to close the file on Ahi Island.

With relief he finished the last notation, then slipped the entire folder into his file drawer. He took a key from his wallet and locked the drawer.

With luck it would not have to be taken out again for another thirty years.

-Two-

Kaimu Kumukahi was glad that the smoke had disappeared and that once again he could surf off Nalowale Island. It would not be long before he had to leave Nalowale for the mainland. His surfing days would be suspended for a while, so he had to make the most of them. He lay on his stomach, paddling out to the open water beyond the dead coral reef where the bottom of the ocean dropped suddenly and the waves were best. His olive-brown skin glistened with salt water and his wet black hair clung to his head and neck. Clad only in bright green shorts he reverently placed an ancient Hawaiian good luck charm around his neck. He was very competitive and his muscular body reflected the many long hours of outdoor events he had participated in.

He saw the wave from afar and watched the roll grow as it came closer. Expertly, he timed his movements to coincide with it, turning first so that he faced the shore, next rising to his knees, and then standing up just as the full power of the wave began to swell under the board. Not even Neptune ever relished his power over the ocean more than Kaimu Kumukah as he rode the wave toward the reef.

Exhilarated when he hit the shore, he decided to go

out again. He stood for a minute looking out at the ocean. Far off to the right he could see the dark shadow of Ahi Island, silent once again. The rest of the vista was undisturbed. He entered the water and began to paddle out.

Once past the reef he noticed some seaweed clinging to the end of his board. He attempted to brush it off with his hand, but to his surprise he couldn't. Instead the wet green tentacle wrapped itself tightly around his finger. Startled, he tried to use his other hand, not wanting to lose his grip on his board. Still on his stomach he again tried to free his entangled hand. Moving so that his face was on his hand, he tried to pull off the constricting tentacle with his strong teeth.

Another large green tentacle gave him a cold wet slap across the face. Startled, he dropped the tentacles from his teeth and tried to raise his head. But he could not lift it. Something cold and wet was holding him down. He struggled with all his might to pull away, but only succeeded in losing his grip on his board. Now he was totally engulfed in the huge mass of green plant tentacles that held him in a deadly embrace. As they tightened around his body he struggled to breathe, gulping salty water. Filled with disbelief he sank below the sea.

The boy and girl drew their outrigger canoe up on the black-and-purple lava coast of the island. They jumped out and walked up to the shore. The young man was about a head taller than the girl and they were both barefoot. Their skin was brown and their hair black and silky. The boy's hair came to his neck, the girl's fell to her waist. She was wearing a bright yellow sarong, and tucked behind her ears were two of the huge new white hibiscus flowers that were growing near the black beach.

He was wearing cut-off jeans and a knife was tucked in at his waist.

The island made the girl nervous. She could remember the way it had looked only a few months ago when the volcano had come to life. The flames and tremors were gone now, the lava beneath their bare feet had hardened to rough blue-black rock, and the air was still thick with the smell of sulfur. Compared to Nalowale it was ugly and gloomy. Malie could not understand why Makani had insisted they come.

He had run a few feet ahead of her and was standing on a pile of boulders, smiling triumphantly. He reached down, taking her hand to steady her as she joined him on top of the rock. As soon as she stood there she saw why he was smiling.

"Oh, Makani," she gasped. "I see it but I don't believe it. It's beautiful. How can this be?"

"I don't know," Makani answered. "Maybe it's a gift from the gods."

Beneath them, at the heart of the dark desolate little island, lay a small lush grove surrounded by palm trees. Huge flowers of pink, purple, red, and white seemed to be everywhere. Yet only a few feet away volcanic ash covered the rest of the island.

They made their way down the other side of the boulder and headed toward the grove. The smell of sulfur had faded, replaced by the fragrant scent of the flowers. Two small white doves cooed as they flew by, as if to welcome them. The only other sound was the rustle of the palms.

"What did I tell you, Malie?" Makani said as he reached up for a bright yellow papaya that was as big as his head. Taking the knife he skillfully broke the heart-shaped fruit in two. He handed half to Malie and she began to suck the orange pulp. "We didn't need to bring any food with us."

Finished, she wiped the juice from her face with a leisurely gesture. "What else are you hiding here, Makani?"

"Follow me." Taking her hand he led her deeper into the trees, so dense in spots that there seemed to be no air or light at all. They came to a clearing at last, or at least the ground was clear, although the sky was almost completely obscured by the leaves of palm trees that seemed to create a dark green canopy. Several plum trees were heavy with purple fruit; only these plums were as big as Makani's fist. Thick new bushes circled the entire grove. They had no flowers but their triangulated leaves were almost as pretty. The little ground not covered by flowers or new plants was still hard black lava. Makani watched Malie dance lightly around the grove. "It's our special place, Malie," he announced. "No one else knows about it."

The girl smiled and then yawned. Makani was so smart. He would make a good husband and their life together would be good. Just the way he had found this beautiful place proved it. No one else would believe them when she described it, she was sure. That was all right, it would be their secret. Someday they would bring their children here. She stepped up on her toes to kiss Makani. He brushed aside the hair from her neck and accidentally knocked the white flowers from her hair.

Laughing, they knelt to pick them up. Now Makani too yawned.

"Are you tired?" Malie asked him.

"Yes," he admitted, sitting beside her on the grass. "Let's stay here awhile and take a nap."

She agreed and together they lay on a bed of flower petals near one of the new odd plants.

As they slept they did not notice the leaves overhead rustle just the slightest bit, shutting out the last bit of light and air. The grove was silent and the air became heavy and they fell into endless sleep.

-Three-

JUNE 2006

Tom Jenson stood in the lanai of his house and watched the evening sun set on Nalowale Island. He was a light-haired man with a neatly trimmed beard, and the strong Hawaiian sun had browned his skin a copper color. His blue eyes sparkled like the Pacific. He wore no shirt, only faded white Levis and sandals and a machete tucked in at his waist.

Just two months ago the eruptions on Ahi had threatened the entire island. Now a peaceful calm reigned. On this July night the boys of Nalowale were riding the last waves before sundown off the coast of the white beach.

Casual visitors to Hawaii might learn that besides the eight major islands there were 124 islands and atolls, but few would ever visit them. Many of them, like Ahi, were untouched by "progress," uninhabitable. Nalowale was an exception since it was home to thirty Hawaiian families and Tom Jenson. The nearest important island was Kaui, and that was 110 miles away.

Like Niihau, Nalowale was privately owned. New England Congregationalist missionaries, who brought civilizing influences such as muumuus to the native

Hawaiians, had first settled it. But in 1867, Mr. and Mrs. Johnathan Wellinton, a jaunty New England couple, purchased it. They fell in love with the beauty of the island and resolved to bring up their children in Rousseau-like simplicity there. Mrs. Wellinton's income from family lumber holdings amounted at the time to $75,000 a year, which could buy a lot of simplicity. They had planned a sugar plantation but there was not enough rainfall.

The island was still owned by their descendants, but they had long ago opted for the simplicity of life in Malibu and Monte Carlo. The villagers of Nalowale let their cows graze on the former estate of the Wellinton family.

Nalowale was a seventy-square-mile island, formed, like the rest of Hawaii, by volcanic eruptions. It was triangular, one side being quite high and dropping eight hundred feet into a lagoon below. The other two sides were low lying. The west or white beach faced toward the mainland, while the east or black beach, so-called because the sand was actually black lava, faced the volcanic island of Ahi. A great coral reef, home to shell-fish and lobster, semi-circled the island about twenty feet from each beach.

There was no place for an airplane to land, Tom's jeep was one of the few cars, and visitors were not encouraged. There were no policemen and no telephones.

The thirty houses, including Jenson's own, were owned by the Wellington family. They had electricity but no indoor plumbing. Most of them were clustered around a sort of square that had once held an altar to Pele, goddess of volcanoes. It looked a little like the New England town where he grew up. His own house sat on a plateau halfway up the mountain and had an excellent view of the sea.

Although the native Nalowalens left the island for high school, and sometimes college or military service, many of them returned. Life on Nalowale was good. The fish were abundant; the fruit and vegetables barely needed to be cultivated, and the weather hardly varied. It was always summer on Nalowale.

Jenson's house had belonged to a plantation caretaker when there was a plantation. It was cozy and had three bedrooms, although in the two years he had been on Nalowale he had never had any guests. It was furnished mostly with old-fashioned wicker and Victorian pieces, most of which had probably come with the first Congregationalist missionaries and survived a hundred years of upheavals political and volcanic. What had once been a dining room was now the radio room, part of the Hawaiian Emergency Radio Network, an interlacing radio system used to broadcast weather warnings to remote islands and ships at sea. Jenson had installed a small eight-power telescope, and had passed many relaxing hours surveying the paradise that surrounded him. He had watched anxiously the eruption on Ahi Island and was greatly relieved when it fell quiet again.

During the volcano alert, Jenson had been at the radio almost constantly, afraid even to go to the bathroom for fear he would miss some news. The greatest fear was that the volcano eruption would be followed by a tidal surge, but none came. The villagers looked after him, sending their children with gifts of fruit and drink, almost like offerings to a god. In a way their lives had depended on him if only for a few weeks. He did not like the feeling. He had not come to Nalowale to be anyone's god.

Tonight Nalowale looked the way it had when he first saw it. The white beach sparkled in the setting sun; the blue waves beckoned. Fruit was ripening in the trees, begging to be picked. For a few weeks after he had arrived he even believed he could live off the land, reaching up for a ripe papaya whenever he got hungry. It did not work out exactly like that but he had been lucky enough to get a job operating and maintaining the small island radio transmitter that linked Nalowale and the other remote islands with headquarters in Honolulu.

The Nalowalens made him feel welcome. They asked no questions about where he had been or where he was going. That was good, since he did not know himself.

Two years had flown and he had no intention of ever leaving. There was nothing for him on the mainland now.

He looked up and smiled as a small suntanned boy approached the lanai. Like most of the villagers Keoni was a pure Hawaiian with light-brown skin and round eyes that were almost as black as his straight dark hair. He was carrying a large basket of fruit and smiling broadly.

"What've you got there, Keoni?" Jenson asked. The boy was twelve years old, but more mature than a mainland boy his age. He was sure he wanted to operate the island radio just like Jenson when he grew up.

"I picked a mango for you," Keoni said eagerly. "Look at this." He held out the largest mango that Jenson had ever seen. It was easily the size of a watermelon, but it had the distinctive pear shape and red skin of a ripe mango.

Jenson started to laugh at the ridiculous size of the fruit, but when he saw the wounded look in Keoni's eyes he cut it short. “Let's see how it tastes,” he said, and taking a knife he split the fruit in two. It had rich juicy orange pulp inside and after removing the large pit he handed half back to the boy.

Together they sucked noisily on the fruit, sticky juice dripping from their lips and chins. There was so much fruit that Jenson thought for a minute he might not be able to finish it. When he finally did he grinned back at Keoni.

“Good?” Keoni asked.

“Delicious. Where'd you find it?”

“They're growing like this all over the black beach,” the boy said. “Not just mangoes. Breadfruit, coconuts, everything.”

That was good news. But plants were nothing if not adaptable. Not like human beings. Once in school a teacher of his had announced to the class that if every human being disappeared tomorrow it would not affect plant life in the least. But if every plant disappeared mankind could not survive. It had something to do with the oxygen they produced.

Well, Nalowale was evidently safe. If these plants continued growing at this rate they would have oxygen to spare.

“Keoni! Keoni!” A woman's voice was calling outside. As Jenson looked out he realized how suddenly it had become dark.

It was nine o'clock.

“Is that your mom?” he asked.

“Yeah.” The boy shrugged. “I got to get home. She doesn't like me to bother you.”

"You're no bother," Jenson assured him. "Come anytime."

He watched the boy from the doorway and waved at Mrs. Taal, a stout but still attractive woman in a bright yellow muumuu. She waved back and he noticed that she was wearing a huge red hibiscus flower in her long black hair. So the flowers on Nalowale were thriving too.

His thoughts were interrupted by a beeping signal from the radio. He sat down at the transmitter but midway through the routine update of weather conditions he realized with irritation that he was still getting interference. Damn. He'd been tinkering with the blasted thing for two days and it was still there. It was his turn now to broadcast the news to three key points on nearby islands. If there were an emergency, like another volcanic eruption, the job would be crucial. But tonight he was not telling them anything that even Keoni could not tell from a glance at the stars, a walk on the beach, and a deep breath of salt air. It was another peaceful night in paradise.

Kaimu Keoniiah's body was washed up on the white beach at dawn the next morning. Jenson was the first to see it when he completed the 6 a.m. report and went to the water for a swim before breakfast. The boy's body was unmarked, and at first Jenson thought he was sleeping, but as he came closer he noticed the swelling, the awful distortion of the face, like some horrible mask--and the flies.

He knelt down on the wet sand and turned the boy over. He knew it was Kaimu by the pendant around his neck. The last time they had talked the boy had explained how lucky it was. Well, it had not brought poor Kaimu much luck. Suddenly he wanted to cry, but instead he forced himself to take deep breaths as he gently lifted the boy's body in his arms and carried it up to the lanai where he laid it on the couch. It would be safe there from the wild dogs and whatever else was out there

As much as he was a part of the island community he did not relish the idea of telling Kaimu's parents that their son was dead. Instead, he went looking for Keoni's father, the nominal headman of the island. He found him outside his house, under the shade of a rainbow shower tree, preparing his nets for fishing. "Aloha," he greeted the man who looked like an older, plumper version of Keoni. He had the same brown skin and black hair and eyes. Like Jenson his chest was bare and he wore cotton jeans. His gestures were almost elegant as he worked over the nets.

"Aloha, Tom," Kuahiwi responded; then noticed the grave look on Jenson' face, "Is something wrong?"

"Yes. I found Kaimu." In a village the size of Nalowale everyone went by first names, just as everyone knew when someone was missing. And Kaimu had been missing for three days.

"Dead?"

Jenson nodded. "I brought him back to my house, out of the way of the wild animals," he said. "I thought you should tell his parents."

"Yes." Kuahiwi put aside his nets. He would not be fishing today. "Do you know what happened?"

Jenson rubbed his beard thoughtfully. "I suspect he drowned, although it seems strange, a kid like that, swimming like a fish all his life."

"Kaimu was the strongest boy on Nalowale,"

Kuahiwi said firmly, as he looked out toward the dark specter of Ahi.

"Do you have another idea?" Jenson asked.

The older man shook his head. "No, it's just that the boy was a good swimmer. And Makani and Malie are missing, you know."

"No, I didn't know." But that was different. The young couple had probably slipped away for a romantic interlude and would be back in a few days. "You were young once, weren't you, Kuahiwi?"

Kuahiwi shrugged. "The Kona is blowing today," he said softly. "That wind never brings any good." He stood up.

"Kuahiwi, with your permission, I'd like to arrange an autopsy for the boy."

"And if we refuse?"

"I don't want to force you or the boy's family to go against your beliefs, Kuahiwi, but you yourself said the death was unusual.

Kuahiwi nodded. "You arrange your autopsy; I'll take care of Kaimu's family."

The Oahu medical examiner in Honolulu had never been happy with the traditional way Nalowale Island handled births and deaths and he was only too pleased to send out a boat for Jenson. His autopsy report came via the radio the following morning.

"I've got the report on an autopsy on your adolescent Hawaiian male," the disinterested voice of the Oahu operator came across the wire.

"Go ahead," Jenson ordered.

"Well, it's death by suffocation," he continued reading from the report.

Jenson hit the table in disgust. He did not need to waste anyone's time if that was the case. He was so angry he almost forgot about the operator.

"There's more," the voice crackled.

"Go ahead."

"Well, he didn't drown. He suffocated all right, but there was no salt water in his lungs." For once the voice showed interest. "Hey, didn't you say you found the kid in the water?"

"The beach," Jenson said curtly and then signed off. He had no desire to prolong a conversation with this ghoul on Oahu.

He walked to the lanai and stared out at the beach. The bougainvillea vines had grown tall in the last few weeks and now they were reaching for the roof of the house. The scent of the purple and lavender flowers was heavy in the air.

The report bothered him. It bothered him a great deal. A boy had smothered in the Pacific Ocean. There was something very wrong about that, but he could not pinpoint what it was. He decided to take a walk to get his mind off the disturbing news and he headed for the small cluster of wooden houses less than a mile from his own.

Ten white clapboard houses encircled what passed for Nalowale's town square. But at the center of the square was a remnant of ancient Hawaii: a massive stone altar on which ancestors of the Nalowalens had once sacrificed human beings to pacify an angry volcano goddess on Ahi. Nearby was the largest house; it belonged to the Maori family who operated a general store on the lanai. It was also a good place to find some company and pick up the news. He headed for the front door.

"Aloha, Tom." The young Hawaiian woman smiled when he walked in. She was wearing a loose red-flowered muumuu and eating one of the big new mangoes.

"Aloha, Lani," he said. "How's the baby?"

"Fine," she said, patting her belly. "He's starting to kick me."

"He probably wants more mangoes," he joked. "Did you bring that back from the black beach?

"No." She shook her head. "Now our mangoes are just as big." She pointed to a pile of fruit in a bowl. Each green-and-red fruit was the size of a large cantaloupe.

The walls of the small verandah were lined with shelves and on the shelves were a mixed bag of package goods that included Ivory soap, Wise potato chips, and Prince Albert tobacco. Lani and her husband made a tidy profit bringing these goods in from the mainland.

He helped himself to a can of the tobacco and put it on the counter that separated him from Lani.

"Anything else?" she asked.

"No, thanks" he said, taking out a five-dollar bill. "Any news about Makani and Malie?"

Lani shook her pretty head. She was not much older than Malie and they had been good friends.

"I don't understand those two," she said. "Why would anyone want to leave Nalowale?"

Why indeed, Jenson wondered as he took up his change and headed outside. It was almost noon and most of the men were out fishing. The women all waved to him and greeted him by name as he passed. Even after the years he had been on Nalowale they were still curious about him, he realized, still puzzled by his solitary life. Suddenly he heard Keoni's voice.

"Hey, Tom," the boy shouted as he passed. "Can I come help you with the radio?"

Jenson smiled. For some reason he welcomed company this morning, even Keoni's. Besides, the boy was a good pupil and he liked the idea of having someone else able to handle the radio just in case something ever happened to him.

"Sure," he said. "Come on back with me." The boy stepped in next to him and chattered about the big new fruits, the fish, and the upcoming luau all the way back to the house.

It was exactly twelve o'clock when they arrived and Jenson immediately sat down at the radio. It was time to make his regular air check. As soon as he began, he knew there was trouble.

"Damn," he whispered softly.

"What's the matter?" the boy asked. "Are we getting interference again?"

"I'm afraid so, pal," Jenson admitted. "It's that crazy signal again."

"What do you think it is, Tom?"

Jenson shook his head. "I've got no idea. But we can't go on like this; that's for sure. With this kind of interference, all we need is one good typhoon and Ahi and every plane and ship in the area is going to be totally incommunicado."

"Wow! I guess that would be bad," whispered the boy.

Jenson did not hear him. He was listening grimly to the intense crackle of whatever it was that was slowly obscuring every radio message he tried to send or receive.

-Four-

Mike Ryan was sitting at his desk at the Pacific Center Radio office in Honolulu. The scarred oak desk was covered with photographs and a map of the remote islands of the Hawaiian archipelago.

He had been in the business for the last thirty years and had operated everything from a ham radio to satellite systems. He was the ideal man to supervise the state of the art emergency radio network and he knew it. Even with sophisticated weather-monitoring technology the remote Hawaiian Islands were dependent on his emergency network. The system had really paid for itself many times over and was mainly responsible for the fact that since 1946 not one life had been lost in a tidal wave in Hawaii.

Ryan was a big, broad-chested man of fifty-five. Most of the original flaming red hair had given way to gray, but there was plenty of heat still in the oven. With his love of company and outgoing nature he was an exception to the usual radio operator.

Most of the men who operated the transmitting stations were loners, eager to leave something--or more often someone--behind. After a year they got it out of their systems and were ready to go back to life on the mainland.

What Mike could not understand was a guy like Tom Jenson who had settled down on Nalowale as if it were real life. Not that it was any of his business, but still. He had heard the guy's family was loaded, that he had gone to Harvard or Yale or something. And there he was, living on breadfruit and coconuts on Nalowale. Go figure.

He had been thinking about Jenson because he had been the first to report interference: some kind of oddball signal fluctuating all over the net. He had kidded him about cleaning his equipment, but they both knew Jenson was too responsible a guy to get sloppy. No, if he was reporting interference, then something was interfering.

It would be nice to dismiss it as just a lot of seaweed, but Hawaii was of strategic importance to the United States in the Pacific. Anything that interfered with the operation of military and naval equipment interfered with national defense. And now two navy warships, the aircraft carrier USS *Defiant* and the destroyer USS *Wyoming* had reported the same interference.

And there was more. He had been particularly warned to watch the Ahi area during the volcanic activity and he had been making daily reports to the Kaolani Center during the crisis. Nothing had happened, but now he wondered if Dr. Fleming at the center had been expecting this interference all along.

One thing was for sure; Nalowale was a remote island and if the communications broke down, especially during the high storm season, it could be disastrous. So they had to locate the source of that interference, and soon.

Methodically he listed the things that the island had in common with the two ships reporting trouble. There was nothing interesting there. Next he took the map of the South Pacific, noted the positions of the ships when they reported trouble, and marked Jenson's location on Nalowale. Then, taking a ruler he began to draw lines through the points, forming a triangle. Just as he expected, smack in the middle of the triangle was Ahi Island.

Something on Ahi was transmitting a signal. But that was ridiculous. Ahi had been inactive for a hundred years and, if any life had managed to scrape out an existence on the dried lava, it would have been wiped out when the volcano exploded. Maybe it was just some kid with a radio of his own. But the kid must be a prodigy because those signals were awfully strong.

He took out a yellow legal pad and began to draft his report to Dr. Fleming, recommending that Ahi Island be investigated as soon as possible.

-Five-

At the Kaolani Center, Dr. Richard Fleming watched his two young assistants as they finished reading the report from Mike Ryan. His office was in a penthouse atop the center building and had two large windows that overlooked the manicured grounds of the center. On the walls were huge photographs of the active volcanoes of Hawaii. Ahi, which had been a total surprise, had only recently been added. But no one was looking outside or at the photographs now.

Fleming had never married and he regarded these two young scientists as his own children. Ian Evans at twenty-six was tall and sandy-haired with dark-brown eyes and an intense, sometimes abrasive, manner. In time, Fleming hoped, he would lose his rough edges and complete the promising research he had begun on the sensitivity of plants. There was no doubt, however, about Deborah Saunders' fulfilling her promise. The tall blonde Midwesterner had been with the center less than a year but she had already proven herself one of the most capable botanists he had ever worked with. At twenty-four, she had published several major papers on plant life and her research into the "greenhouse effect" was considered seminal.

"Well, what do you think?" Fleming asked when they had finished reading the report.

"It's all very interesting, but hardly something to concern us," Evans said coolly. "Now, if you don't mind, I'd like to get back to the lab." He started to rise from his leather chair, but Fleming motioned for him to remain seated.

"It's not as simple as that, Ian," he said. "First, let's hear from Deborah."

"Well," Deborah began slowly, "I have to admit I'm interested in the idea of the interference coming from Ahi. Now that we know for sure that this isn't accidental interference, I'm more curious than ever. Whatever is sending out those signals is awfully powerful. And yet, as far as we know, nothing exists on that island."

"You've got Nalowale a few miles away," Evans snapped. "There are plenty of people there. Some of them probably set up a ham radio and they're jamming everything in sight."

"Ian, do you seriously believe that an amateur radio operator could send out a signal powerful enough to disrupt communication from two navy warships?" Dr. Fleming asked patiently. "Perhaps he or she could manage such a feat once or twice, probably by accident, but this is appearing on a continuing basis. And it's strong, very strong."

"Sure, maybe the Japanese are planning another invasion," Evans said sarcastically. "And they picked scenic Ahi Island for their first stop. None of those messy ships around like at Pearl."

Deborah Saunders stared at him. Ian Evans's rudeness never ceased to surprise her, but Dr. Fleming just ignored it.

"A scientist must be open to every possibility, Ian, and I think that another transmitter is a possibility that should be investigated. I want you and Deborah to go out there tomorrow in the center launch. Plan on spending a few days there. Jenson, the radioman, can put you up. Take all the equipment you think you'll need. I want to know what's causing that interference on Ahi.

"Can't this wait?" Evans asked. He was obviously not looking forward to an indefinite stay on a remote island. "I'm in the middle of an important experiment."

"Have you ever bothered with an unimportant experiment, Ian?" Fleming smiled. "I'm surprised at you. Where is your scientist's curiosity?"

Deborah and Ian rose to leave and as soon as they were in the hall, he began to complain.

"This is outrageous," he insisted. "He's only sending us out there because he feels threatened by my work."

"Oh, really, Ian, where's your scientist's curiosity?" Deborah countered. She was used to Evans's complaints about Dr. Fleming. He made no secret of the fact that he wanted Fleming's job.

Still, it was odd to be sending both of them out on such a routine mission. Ian could easily have checked out the interference alone. For that matter, so could she. But it was foolish to try to second-guess a genius like Richard Fleming. She had only been at the center less than a year, and in that time he had taught her more about the secrets of plants than all the teachers and scientists she had ever known. She had been surprised at first, when Dr. Fleming had invited her to join the staff of Kaolani Center. After all, she was a trained botanist, but she knew nothing about volcanoes. Then Dr. Fleming explained about his interest in the effects of volcanoes on the vegetation of Hawaii and how important it was.

The invitation to join the center could not have come at a better time. Teaching botany at the University of Chicago had not been the greatest job in the world, but she had stayed on just to be with Chad. Chad Sayers was a brilliant scientist and to be his assistant and intimate was a wonderful life. In their two years together, Chad always came first. He had asked her to marry him many times, but she had always refused.

"My parents were married and miserable," she had said. "My mother said the only piece of paper that brought them any happiness was their divorce decree." That statement had made her ever more cautious.

Then suddenly Chad announced he was taking a job at Harvard and he was going alone.

"I'm sorry, Debbie," he told her. "We've had a good time, but I need a commitment, and if you can't make it, maybe it's because we're not right for each other after all."

Even now, a year later, recalling those words filled her with pain. The only way she could forget about Chad and Chicago was to concentrate on her work at the institute. And there was plenty of work. Like these strange new signals that Mike Ryan had traced to Ahi Island.

"Any plans for dinner?" Ian was asking her. "We can plan our strategy for this field trip."

She shook her head. "No, thanks, Ian. I want to pack and read up on the island." Besides, she knew from experience that dinner with Ian would end up with the usual proposition that they join forces to overthrow Dr. Fleming. The pass that went with it was almost incidental.

She was not interested in either. She did not need Ian Evans to convince her that she was an attractive and desirable woman and when it came to unseating Dr. Fleming, as far as she was concerned Ian was not fit to wash out the doctor's test tubes.

-Six-

Jenson was waiting on the beach at four in the afternoon when the Kaolani Institute's new jet-drive research launch skimmed across the water at fifty miles an hour and docked at the white beach. He grinned when he saw Mike Ryan get off.

A young good-looking man and woman, both wearing dark navy-blue jump suits, followed him off the boat. Mike introduced them as Dr. Deborah Saunders and Dr. Ian Evans. The woman removed her glasses to shake hands. She had dark-blue eyes and a no-nonsense grip. Her pale blonde hair was pulled back in a bun and she wore gold gypsy hoops in her ears, but no make-up. The man's grip was clammy and limp, but his manner was intense. Jenson sensed there was going to be trouble there.

"You can leave your equipment on the launch," he told them. "We'll be taking it out again later anyway." Evans bristled. "This is very valuable equipment, Mr. Jenson, some of it is one of a kind."

Jenson grinned, his white teeth shining against his dark tanned face. "Maybe it's valuable to someone on the mainland, sir, but I don't think it would help any of us catch any more fish, thank you." It was guys like Evans who reminded him why he had come to Nalowale.

Evans just ignored him and pointedly locked the cabin of the launch. Jenson had never seen anyone lock up a boat before. He drove them up about a quarter-mile from the beach to a lovely white house. A spacious lanai was covered with bougainvillea; the purple-and-magenta flowers were as big as a man's hand.

"Oh, I had no idea!" Deborah exclaimed. Jenson laughed. "I guess you were expecting a grass shack, weren't you?"

"Yes," she admitted. "And I'm amazed at the size of the flowers."

"It's like this all over the island," Jenson said.

Inside, his house was sparsely furnished with wicker and Victorian pieces. Deborah noticed with surprise that he had a large collection of books on shelves in the living room: titles by Melville, Thoreau, and Emerson. It was not what she was expecting from a professional beachcomber.

"Ryan and Dr. Evans can share a room, and this here is yours," Jenson said, indicating a small room almost filled by a narrow brass bed and a large Victorian bureau. It could have been a room in a Massachusetts farmhouse except for the view of the blue Pacific and a vine of white bougainvillea and red hibiscus that framed it

"Thank you," she said. "Now, can you tell me where the shower is?"

Jenson laughed again. He seemed to find everything she said amusing and it made her uncomfortable.

"I don't see what's so funny," she said somewhat haughtily.

"I'm afraid our plumbing is a little primitive

compared to Honolulu, Dr. Saunders," he said. His blue eyes were sparkling with suppressed laughter. "There's a shower out back with a barrel of rain water next to it; just hook it up to the pipes. And the facilities are just about five feet further from the house."

She winced. "The facilities?"

"Yes, ma'am."

"Well," she sighed, "I guess I can get used to it; I'm not here on vacation."

As he turned away and left her to her unpacking she realized that the room was full of the heady fragrance of the oversize flowers. In such beautiful surroundings it was going to be hard to remember that she was here on a scientific mission. Even Jenson was a surprise. She had pictured a grizzled old hermit and he had turned out to be handsome and even friendly, at least to her. Unfortunately, she was afraid that the little flare-up about locking the cabin of the launch was not going to be the last between Ian Evans and Tom Jenson.

After showing the two men to their room, Jenson laid out some roast breadfruit and coconut wine for his guests and waited for them on the lanai. Ryan was the first to join him.

"You were right about those plants, Tom," Ryan said as he sat down on the wide couch Hawaiians call a hiklee. "I've never seen anything like this."

"Yes," Jenson agreed. "They started up right about the same time as the interference on the radio."

"So, you're still getting that?" Ryan helped himself to a large piece of the breadfruit.

"Yes, it scatters across the entire bandwidth and it's affecting all frequencies."

Jenson reached for the calabash in which he kept the wine and poured himself and Ryan generous glassfuls.

"Well, pal," Ryan said as he raised his glass, "you're not alone. The *Defiant* and the *Wyoming* both reported the same problem when they were on maneuvers off Ahi. Screwed-up instruments; magnetic interference; everything. Nobody can put a finger on it, except that now I'm really sure the signal, whatever it is, is coming from the island."

"That seems awfully strange," Jenson said, shaking his head.

"Maybe, pal. But somebody is sending a signal from there and when we find the guy I'm going to have to explain the facts of life and FCC licenses to him. You can't just set up a competing radio system that screws up the Hawaiian emergency network and the navy without attracting some trouble for yourself."

"What makes you so sure it's somebody?"

Ryan shrugged. "The signal's too strong to be accidental. Somebody's deliberately using our airwaves and it's got to stop. When we find that transmitter on Ahi I'm going to take great pleasure in dismantling it."

But Jenson had other things on his mind besides the strange signals. "Mike, how much do you know about the Kaolani Center?"

"What's to know? They get a lot of government money to observe volcanoes and I get a little government money to alert them about anything unusual about volcanoes." Ryan drained his glass and helped himself to more wine. "You know, Tom, you could develop a taste for this stuff."

“Come on, Mike,” Jenson persisted. “I know why you're here. But what about the whiz kids? What are they here for?”

“They want to get a look at Ahi,” Ryan said. “Just in case the signals are connected to the volcano somehow.”

It must be nice to feel as secure as Ryan, Tom thought. The Kaolani Center wanted reports, so he sent them reports. It was as simple as that. Like so many people he had known in his life, Ryan had great respect for science. Jenson’s own respect had fallen a long time ago; in fact, it had sunk to the bottom of a lake, along with the rest of his dreams. He had turned his back on most of the twentieth century and come to Nalowale to get as far away from the vain hopes and dreams of science as he could.

They were all alike, the scientists, convinced they had all the answers. Ian Evans was typical, and he would have recognized him anywhere. The woman was different, softer, and quieter. But appearances were deceiving, as deceiving as dormant volcanoes.

“All ready?” Ryan asked, rising from the couch as Evans and Deborah Saunders came out to the lanai. She had pulled her long blond hair back into a ponytail and had changed into a pair of shorts and a flowered T-shirt. She had excellent legs, Jenson noticed, although he could not have explained why that surprised him.

“Well, come on, let's go,” Evans said anxiously. Jenson avoided pointing out that Ahi Island was not going anywhere. There was something about his tone that Jenson did not like. Evans made it clear that he regarded him and Ryan harmless yokels.

“We were only waiting for you, Dr Evans,” he said

dryly. He turned away, and they followed him to the jeep and drove down to the beach and the waiting launch.

Jenson had barely noticed the boat when it arrived but now he took a closer look. It was a luxury boat, slightly larger than a large yacht and fitted with everything from a telephone to a deep freeze.

"Ever sail one of these babies?" Ryan asked as they boarded the ship. He would be in command on the water, and he seemed to relish being behind the captain's wheel.

"No," Jenson admitted.

"It's a beauty. And that cabin below looks like something out of Star Wars."

"Yes," Dr. Saunders agreed. "Dr. Fleming is very proud of the lab. It's almost as well equipped as the original back at the center."

Ryan started up the launch and it cut smoothly through the blue water as it headed toward the dark ominous specter of Ahi.

"Have you ever been on a volcanic island, Dr. Saunders?" Jenson asked casually. "There's not much to see, you know. The last time I was on Ahi, right after the final eruption, it looked like a moonscape. Three feet of hot lava and ash everywhere you looked."

"I'm not here for the scenery, Mr. Jenson," she cut him off stiffly. "Dr. Evans and I want to find the source of the interference you're getting."

"And so you will," Jenson agreed, but Deborah had the uncomfortable feeling that he found both Evans and herself highly amusing. She did not have time to be annoyed, though, because the black mountain of lava was coming into view. It was majestic: a brooding blot against the pristine blue of the sky and water.

Mike moored the launch off a huge pumice boulder several yards from the shore and they waded through the shallow water to the beach carrying Evans's tracking equipment high above their heads.

The lava shore had hardened into blue and black rock. Deborah was surprised to see that some grass and a few scrubby ferns had already begun to spring up on the lava. It usually took many years for even the hardiest plants to reestablish themselves on new lava. Otherwise the island reminded her of Kahoolawe, the barren little island used by the military for target practice not far from Nalowale. But that particular patch of ugliness was man-made. Ahi was entirely a creation of nature.

"That's odd," she said, staring at a particularly leafy little fern.

"What's that?" Ian asked.

"This fern," she said as she bent down to break off a leaf. "This must be a very hardy little plant to have put down roots here so soon after an eruption. I'd like to take a look at it in the lab."

"That's real nice, Deborah," Evans said impatiently. "But in case you've forgotten, we're supposed to be here to track down that transmitter."

"No problem," Jenson interjected. "You and Mike can work on one side of the island and Dr. Saunders and I will take the other. We should be done in two hours, the island's not that big, and we'll meet you both back at the boat at five o'clock."

"Okay," Evans agreed reluctantly. "Come on, Mike."

Jenson watched them walk away and then turned to Deborah. "I don't think he wants to leave me alone with you." Again he seemed amused.

"Oh, don't pay attention to Ian. He's so anxious to make a name for himself as a great scientist that he's terrified someone else might attract more attention."

"Well, let's get started then." He smiled and pointed toward a large pumice boulder. Walking toward it they both saw the huge plant growing beside it.

It had a wide cluster of long rigid leaves pointing upward. At the center of the leaves was a tall stalk six feet in the air and lined on all sides from top to bottom with brilliant purple and yellow flowers, each the size of a dinner plate.

"This is very unusual," Deborah said softly as they neared the odd flowers. "A silversword plant like this should take years to develop." She examined some of the silver leaves at the base. "This seems to have matured overnight."

"Look, here's another one," Jenson said. "And it's twice the size of any I've ever seen before." As he stared at the plant he could make out several more nearby. "You know, Dr. Saunders, we've been getting unusually large plants on the east end of Nalowale lately. Just like these flowers."

But she did not hear him; she was running ahead, looking for any other signs of life. Then she saw the trees: tall leafy banana trees surrounding a small grove. She blinked several times, afraid that it was a mirage. But it was no illusion.

"Tom," she called. "Come see this!" She paused on the edge, reluctant to enter the lush green grove alone.

In less than a minute he was beside her. "Out of sight," he muttered. "I'm glad you're here, Deborah. If I'd seen this alone, I would never have believed it."

Together they entered the small oasis. Luscious green plants were everywhere. The banana trees seemed to have grown tall overnight and they were laden with yellow fruit that hung in bunches, each banana at least two feet long. There were several huge bombax trees with pale pink pompom blossoms as big as basketballs. Each flower had a bright pink stamen more than a foot long.

Suddenly Deborah screamed. “Oh, God!”

Jenson came running. The bodies of a Hawaiian boy and girl lay near the shade of a tree. They looked peaceful, as though they were sleeping. The air in the grove was completely still and tasted faintly sour.

“It's Makani and Malie,” he said. “They’re from Nalowale. They've been missing.”

Quickly recovering her composure, Deborah bent down over the bodies and began to examine them with professional detachment. “There are no marks on them,” she announced as she stood back up. Jenson thought of the boy who had drowned. Not drowned, he corrected, himself, smothered.

“I want these bodies autopsied,” he said.

Deborah stared at him and he realized that he had spoken in a loud voice. Good, let her know he meant it. He was beginning to think the Ahi interference was interfering with more than radio waves.

“Of course there'll be an autopsy. We all want to be sure that there's no connection between the death of these children and the signals,” she said, echoing his thoughts.

“Suppose there is a connection,” Jenson said. “Then what?”

“Then it will be dealt with in an appropriate manner,”

she added crisply.

He decided it was ridiculous to stand there discussing it. “Do you suppose you can give me a hand with these bodies?”

Reluctantly she lifted up the body of Malie while Jenson carried Makani back to the waiting boat.

On the other side of the island Ryan and Evans equipped with hand-held ECM counters and digital frequency counters, attempted to locate and identify the transmitter, but unsuccessfully. The signals were still strong though, so Ryan had been right about it coming from Ahi. But where? It seemed as if they had covered the entire island and everywhere they went the signal was the same.

“I don't get it, Mike,” Evans said wearily. “The signal's got to be transmitting from somewhere.”

“It's like the island itself was one big transmitter,” Ryan muttered.

They had been so engrossed in their work that they hardly noticed a stray clump of greenery rooted on a lava ridge.

Suddenly Ryan shouted, “Hey, Ian, look at this!” He had set up his frequency detector at the edge of a clearing. “The digital read-out fluctuated wildly. I've never seen it like this.”

Evans came over to look at the equipment. “What do you make of it?” he asked.

“I think I've got the source.”

“Yeah?” Evans was interested. “What?”

“I can't tell you,” Ryan said excitedly. “Let me show you.

He led him back down to the beach and gestured

toward a clump of short thick bushes with odd triangular leaves, each about the size of a man's hand.

"When the signals started to come in, I moved out into the open. The signal weakened, but as I came in closer where those bushes began to get heavier, so did the signal."

"That's strange," Evans admitted. Maybe it was worth taking a look.

"I started here," Ryan began, anxious to reproduce every detail. "Look, here it goes again."

The read-out had once again begun to fluctuate wildly. "I'll be damned," Evans said.

"Now watch," Ryan said, encouraged. "As I walk away and back toward the beach, the signal fades."

"It sure does," Evans agreed as the numbers began to slow down and seemed hardly to register at all. "Let's take a run back up to the trees and watch the meter."

"There it goes again," Ryan said excitedly. The signal strength increased as they came closer to the plants.

"Now, hold it near this big bush," Evans ordered, indicating one of the new plants with the odd leaves.

He did so. "Look at this, Dr. Evans," he shouted. "The heavy thick clumps are transmitting even more strongly."

The two men stared at each other. Now they were sure that it was the plants. The mysterious transmissions that had been interfering with radio signals in the Ahi area were coming from these odd new plants with the triangular leaves. And neither of them had the slightest idea what that meant.

The silence was broken by the approach of Jenson and Deborah

"Hey, Mike," Jenson called. "Can you give me a hand? We've got a problem." He explained about the bodies of Malie and Makani, hardly mentioning the grove itself.

"The dead can wait, Mr. Jenson," Evans answered for Ryan. "We've got the source of those transmissions."

"Oh, really?" Deborah said with interest. "Where?"

Ryan explained about the radio waves and the odd-looking plants with the triangular leaves. He demonstrated the reaction as he moved the counter closer to the plants.

"I think the next step is to find out what's so special about these plants," Deborah said gravely. "Tom, you've got a knife, can you cut me a piece?"

"Sure." Jenson approached the plant tentatively. He took a heavy branch in his hand and raised his knife.

"Tom," Ryan yelled, "the meter is going wild again!"

Jenson stepped back to look at the meter, but it had returned to normal. "When did it react exactly?" he asked.

"Just when you touched the branch," Ryan said. Then, turning to Ian Evans. "What do you make of that, doc?"

Evans shook his head. "I'm not sure yet, although it looks as if it were reacting to you, Mr. Jenson."

"I want to try something," Jenson said. "Mike, keep your eye on the meter. I'm going to try for a chunk of the branch again. Okay, ready?" Slowly, tentatively, he walked toward the huge bush. None of them spoke; the only sound was the gentle wind and, in the distance, the waves lapping lightly on the hard lava shore. It was so still that the air seemed oppressive and heavy, as though they were inside a bell jar or high atop a mountain. When he was within six inches of the plant he did not hesitate but sliced briskly into the bark.

"There it goes," Ryan called as he watched the readout. Like it's in pain."

Jenson moved quickly, completing the amputation with surgical speed, then turned immediately to the others. "Let's get out of here," he ordered.

It was almost six when Ryan turned the boat back toward Nalowale, and as they sped through the clear blue water, Jenson joined Evans and Deborah on the bow.

Ian Evans was jubilant. "This is the breakthrough I've been waiting for," he said. "Those plants are communicating. They're actually sending out strong enough signals to interfere with our own. They're communicating on our level!"

"But they're not communicating with us, Ian," Deborah cautioned.

"That'll come," he said firmly. "Right now I want to find out just whom they are talking to."

"Meanwhile, what about the interference?" Deborah asked. "We've got to do something about that."

"No problem." Evans grinned. "I'll call Fleming on the launch telephone as soon as we get back. The plants will have to be cut back, but we'll run a simple defoliation of the island. We don't want to wipe out the plants, just cut back on the interference until we break their code."

Deborah stared at the cool blue water. A long-winged sea bird seemed to shear the water with its wings as it flew low on the surface. The bird ignored a large dead grouper that floated by the boat, trailing some thick seaweed. It spoiled the serenity of the water and she turned back to the two men.

"You know," Evans continued, "in 1970 the Agricultural Academy of Moscow suggested that plants have electrical impulses similar to those of nerves in man. They even suggested that plants had a recollection center at the root neck that pulsated like an animal's heart. One of the things they were working on was the possibility that astronauts in space could communicate with each other via plants in their spacecraft if their own electronic systems failed. We've never been able to come close to duplicating those experiments, but these Ahi plants could be the key."

"What is it about Ahi, Dr. Evans?" Jenson asked. "What makes those plants so healthy all of a sudden? Ahi was as close to a desert as something in the South Pacific can be. But that grove looked like a Garden of Eden."

"You know, Mr. Jenson," Evans leaned back in a deck chair and grinned smugly, "I wouldn't be surprised if the signals and the growth are connected in some way."

"The truth is that no one is going to know anything until we look at those plants in the lab," Deborah added.

"And I'm going to check the plants on Nalowale now for signals." Evans laughed. "I don't think that old has-been Fleming knew what he was doing when he sent us here, Deborah. He thought he was getting rid of me and he's practically handed me the scientific discovery of the decade."

With relief Deborah saw that they were about to dock at the quay. The sight of the dead boy and girl had upset her more than she cared to admit.

"Did you happen to notice the air back there?"

Jenson asked casually.

"What about it?" Evans was not particularly interested in anything but his discovery.

"It was heavier, like a steam bath almost."

"Yes, I noticed," Deborah agreed. But Ian brought the subject back to his discovery and she did not pursue it. She could hardly wait to start examining those plant samples in the lab, anything to wipe the picture of Makani and Malie from her mind.

A few hours later, Ian Evans was on the phone to Dr. Fleming on Oahu. Their conversation lasted almost an hour and he did most of the talking. Fleming barely said a word, only grunting occasionally to assure Evans that he was indeed listening to every word. And he was listening intently, scribbling notes furiously as the excited young scientist described the unusual plants on Ahi Island.

"And these plants are responsible for the interference?" Fleming asked when Evans finally finished. "You're quite sure of this?"

"Absolutely," Evans said emphatically. "And the sooner we cut back enough on the plants to eliminate that, the sooner we'll be able to get a handle on the signals. I tell you, Dr. Fleming, we may have found a completely new language here."

"Yes," Fleming agreed.

"So how soon can we defoliate?" Evans wanted to know.

"Immediately, Ian," Fleming said. "I'll arrange to have the area sprayed with Myrozene the day after tomorrow. I'll come out myself," he added.

"Oh, that's not necessary," Evans said hastily.

Fleming smiled to himself. Ian thought he was on the brink of a great discovery and he was reluctant to share the limelight with anyone else. As for himself, he had no particular burning desire to travel out to Ahi and Nalowale, but it had to be done. Ian Evans and Deborah Saunders were on the brink of something, all right, but he suppressed a shudder as he considered the real nature of what that something might be.

-Seven-

The following day, after a breakfast of roast bread-fruit and papaya, Deborah asked Jenson about the big new fruits.

"It's amazing, isn't it?" he said. "Keoni and I picked them all down by the black beach. For some reason the fruit there is the biggest I've ever seen."

"All the fruit?" Deborah asked casually. "Or just the papaya?"

"All of it. Would you like to see?" Jenson asked. "Come on, I'll give you the fifty-cent tour."

She hesitated, torn between professional curiosity and the feeling that Jenson had something besides plants in mind

"You too, Dr. Evans," he added, dispelling her suspicions. "You said you wanted to see if any of the plants here are responding to those signals from Ahi. The black beach is the closest to the island, so they'd be the first to pick up any transmissions."

"What about the radio?" Deborah asked. "Don't you have a call-in schedule?"

"Oh, Mike can take care of that, can't you, Mike?"

"Sure," he said cheerfully. "You guys go ahead. I've seen enough of these islands."

They rose from the table and walked out to Jenson's jeep. No sooner had Tom stepped into it than Keoni appeared. "Hey, Tom," he called. "Where you going? Can I come?"

Jenson turned to the two scientists. "I take the jeep out so seldom that Keoni thinks it's a special occasion. Do you mind if he joins us?"

"Not at all, if he'll give me a hand with the cuttings." Deborah smiled. Jenson could see that Evans was not pleased, but he ignored him.

"I'll get in back," Deborah offered.

"No, no," Keoni insisted, giving Jenson a broad wink. "It's an old Hawaiian custom. Wahinie rides in front."

This was the first Jenson had heard of this old Hawaiian custom, but he said nothing as Keoni climbed into the back seat with Evans. As the jeep moved away from the village square and into the rustic forest, Keoni instantly began a running commentary on the flora and fauna of Nalowale.

"Drive slow," he warned Jenson. "Remember the wild pigs." Suddenly a wild dog scurried across the dirt road and Keoni started to laugh. "Pigs and dogs, everything. It would be nice if they started growing big too."

The dusty unpaved road was lined with tall palm trees, wild ginger, and sugar cane. Beyond them was a forest gone wild, and everywhere the growth was abundant.

"This is a new development," Jenson remarked. "Whatever it is that's making the plants on the black beach grow has spread to here."

"Look at that," Deborah said, pointing at a halapipe

tree with sword-like leaves and brown fruit. "Those berries are the size of plums."

Jenson stopped and she jumped out to cut off a sample. Evans followed with his radio scope.

"It's getting signals," he announced. "And they're coming from the direction of Ahi."

It was like that all the way up the mountain. Every time they stopped at some unusual plant or bush, they found it was receiving signals from Ahi.

"There's no doubt in your mind that the Ahi plants are sending them, is there?" Jenson asked.

"Not a one, pal," Evans said. "The signal is distinct and unique. I'm telling you, this isn't just going to make me director of Kaolani. This is going to get me a Nobel Prize."

Deborah refrained from mentioning that half the work on the project was hers or that Jenson and Ryan were helping them. Jenson stopped the jeep suddenly and pulled it to the side of the road.

"I think we'll proceed on foot from here," he said. "This is the beginning of the rain forest and you really should see it on foot.

The one characteristic of all rain forests is the presence of the endlessly varied ohia lehua. The dark-green foliage and gnarled gray branches were in abundance, growing on top of each other, entwining and rooting upon one another, increasing the density of the forest, and shutting out all but a few rays of sunlight. The air was cool and damp.

Jenson and Keoni strode sure-footedly through the dark wet forest. Deborah followed, impressed by Jenson's obvious familiarity with the place.

"This is incredible," Evans kept yelling from behind. "As the plants receive the harmonic frequency from Ahi, they're responding by growing."

For some reason she could not explain, Deborah wished Ian would stop talking about the plants. Keoni and Jenson were still ahead of her and she ran to catch up. They had stopped and were standing at a clearing and she could not see it until she was on top of them. When she did, the sight almost took her breath away. They had reached the edge of the rain forest and, looking down almost eight hundred feet, she could see the black beach. The ancient lava glittered in the sun with a light that was almost blinding.

"You can see why Captain Cook's sailors thought the coast of Hawaii was loaded with diamonds, can't you?" Jenson remarked. "That's where they got the name for Diamond Head."

"You know a lot about Hawaii, don't you?" she said.

He shrugged. "I live here."

"No," she persisted. "It's more than that. You're really a scholar. I saw your books; I've heard you talk about the islands. Why do you try to pass yourself off as some kind of know-nothing?"

Jenson turned away. Keoni had begun to move down the cliff and he called to him. "Hey, pal. Come on back, we're going to head home now." When he turned back to Deborah she was still staring.

"I'm sorry," she apologized. "I shouldn't have pried, it's my scientist's curiosity; I just wonder why a man like you has buried himself away on Nalowale."

"It's not terribly interesting," he said slowly. "I came here from New England. I grew up there, went to school in Boston, and married a local girl."

"Oh?" She was surprised that this news disappointed her.

"I wanted to live like Thoreau." He smiled, but it was a bittersweet smile as he recalled that long ago year that had begun with such promise. "We had a little house on a lake up there. It was a resort and deserted most of the year. I used to drive thirty miles to work every day to get to my job in Boston, but it was worth it.

"It sounds idyllic," she encouraged him.

"Oh, it was wonderful at first, just the two of us. I had a great job, a beautiful wife. We both thought the lake was an ideal place to live."

Deborah said nothing. She sensed that he had not shared any of this with anyone before and each word seemed to be filled with painful memories.

"Well," he continued, "in 1990 the Gulf War broke out. My naval reserve unit was activated and off I went. Three months later I got a short letter from my wife telling me that she had made a mistake and was going home to reexamine her life."

"I'm sorry," Deborah said softly.

"So was I initially, but as time passed I learned to accept it. Looking back it probably was for the best." He paused as Keoni joined them. "Go ahead, pal, we'll meet you at the jeep."

Keoni grinned, obviously pleased that his friend was deep in conversation with the wahine.

As the boy moved ahead, Jenson returned to his story. "So I quit my job and I came out here. I wanted to get away from all that. And when I got to Nalowale it was completely unspoiled. I guess you see it that way now, but believe me it's changed. Little by little it's losing its innocence." He pointed out to the Pacific, eight hundred feet below. "That coral reef there used to be full of lobster and shellfish, more than enough to support the island. Now there are only a few. It's almost dead."

"What happened?" she asked.

"Time" he said dryly. "More shipping, more tourists, over time it has affected all the water around here."

"I understand why you're so pessimistic," she said. "But I hope that what the Kaolani Center is doing will reverse some of it. That's why Dr. Evans and I are here."

"Oh, really?" he said and his voice sounded skeptical. "I wondered."

"Well, we're really here to examine the volcano and track down that interference," she admitted. "But when I saw those plants growing in the middle of all that new lava and volcanic ash I just knew we were on to something."

"Now you sound like Evans." It was not a compliment.

"I can understand that you as a layman might not be excited about communicating with plants," she said. "But surely even you were impressed with them. If they could grow there they could grow anywhere. Think of what that could mean for the hungry of the world."

"Just what does it mean?" he said dryly. He had had enough of the wonders of science in his life and he did not share her belief in its power for good. Yet he envied her enthusiasm. At least she still believed in something.

"Once we cut back on the plants, so that they stop this interference, we'll be able to set up a lab on the island and watch those plants at every step of their development." Her eyes were shining with thinking of all the possibilities.

"You like your work, don't you?" he said gently.

"Yes," she admitted. "I think that meeting Dr. Fleming was one of the most exciting moments in my life."

"How did you ever hook up with the Kaolani Center?" he asked.

"Oh, it's not a very interesting story." She shrugged. "I was doing some teaching and research at the University of Chicago, nothing spectacular, but I was involved with someone, so I guess I postponed a serious career move. Then we broke up and suddenly I wanted to get away from there so badly I would have taken a job in the Arctic. Fortunately, Dr. Fleming invited me out here."

"And your boyfriend?"

"Ian Evans is not my boyfriend," she said emphatically. It was suddenly very important to make that clear to this man, although she could not explain why. "We both work for Dr. Fleming; that's all we have in common."

Jenson sensed that he had better change the subject.

"What kind of guy is this Dr. Fleming?" he asked.

"He's a genius," she said simply. "He could probably have his own research center anywhere in the world, but he has been a major influence at the Kaolani Center and he cares too much about it ever to leave."

"Sounds like a great guy," Jenson said. He was trying very hard to sound disinterested, but it bothered him to hear the way her voice lilted when she spoke of Dr. Fleming.

"Wait until you meet him," she insisted. "He's going

to supervise the defoliation tomorrow from the *Defiant*, then he'll join us here."

"The *Defiant*?" Jenson repeated. "How did the navy get in on this?"

"You can hardly defoliate an island like Ahi on foot," Deborah said. "If we sent in people on foot they'd all be breathing the poison."

"That's not exactly true, is it?" he said. "Myrozene was developed specifically as a defoliant that would not harm human beings, wasn't it?"

Deborah looked at him, surprised that a layman would know anything about the new defoliant. "You're right," she admitted. "But in the last year we've discovered that it's more dangerous to handle than we'd thought, so we're only using it from the air."

"So, another scientific advance disappears in a mushroom cloud," he said dryly.

"You can't make an omelet without breaking eggs," Ian Evans observed as he and Keoni rejoined them.

Deborah tried to contain her anger by concentrating on deciding whom she disliked more: Ian Evans or Tom Jenson.

It was sundown when they returned to the village, dropped Keoni off at his house, and proceeded to Jenson's house. Ryan was standing in front when the jeep pulled up.

"I've got a surprise for you inside," he announced as they walked in. Sitting on the hikiee was a stout dark man with gray hair dressed in white Levis and sandals and the loudest blue aloha shirt Jenson had ever seen.

"Dr. Fleming," Deborah cried, obviously pleased.

The older man rose and offered his hand. "Mr.

Jenson, I presume?"

Jenson shook hands. "I guess you know everybody else," he said, hiding his surprise. From the way Deborah had talked about him, he had pictured someone more along the lines of James Mason.

"Oh, yes." The older man nodded.

"What are you doing here, Dr. Fleming?" Evans asked. He seemed to be the only one not entirely pleased with the new arrival.

"I was on the *Defiant* arranging the defoliation operation and rather than spend the night on board, I had one of the helicopters bring me here. I wanted a chance to see this outrageous growth myself."

"How lucky for us," Evans said so sarcastically that Deborah glared at him. But Dr. Fleming seemed not to notice.

"You must have a lot of pull, Dr. Fleming, to get the navy to move this fast," Jenson said casually.

This was the second time he had mentioned the navy, Deborah realized.

Fleming shrugged. "At the center we do a lot of consulting work," he explained. "And in this case, they're just as anxious as we are to cut back on the interference. It's awfully hard to navigate when all your equipment is being affected."

"So I hear," Jenson said.

"Where is the *Defiant* now?" Ryan asked.

"Moored about three miles east of Ahi. Their helicopters will take off tomorrow at dawn and we can monitor the operation from here on Mr. Jenson's radio," he said. "Incidentally, the crew of the *Defiant* has not been told anything about the signals and their connection with the interference."

"So they know nothing about the Ahi plants and their signals?" Jenson asked.

"That's right." Fleming nodded. "This kind of thing has a way of getting blown out of all proportion and we don't want that to happen here."

"You mean talking plants might not be so good for the tourist business." Ryan laughed.

"Not only that, I'm afraid," Fleming said. "Until that interference is cleared up planes and ships in this area are in serious danger. We can't possibly guarantee the integrity of their navigational equipment."

"Well, I can guarantee you're going to like my dinner, if you'll come in and start eating," Ryan joked. They sat down at the table where he had laid out a broiled sea trout and thick slices of the fried green bananas called plantains. To his delight the group made short work of the meal, washing it down with plenty of coconut wine. As they finished off the desert of sliced mango and papaya salad, Fleming commented on the size of the fruit.

"Yes," Jenson said. "It started on the east end of the island a month ago. But it's spread over most of the island now. All the fruit trees, all the flowers, everything."

"The east end?" Fleming asked. "Isn't that the point nearest to Ahi?"

"You got it," Evans said eagerly. "And once we start seriously examining the Ahi plants we're going to find out how they do it."

"Do what, Ian?" Deborah asked.

"Get the plants to grow," he almost shouted. "It's

those signals from Ahi. Somehow they're influencing the plants on Nalowale to grow."

"Interesting, if true," Fleming said gravely.

"You bet your life it's true," Evans snapped.

"Well, after tomorrow you'll be able to see for yourselves, won't you?" Jenson said.

They finished in silence, aware that they were on the threshold of a great adventure.

-Eight-

The following morning, Dr. Fleming was the first one up and he decided to take a walk on the beach to clear his head before the operation began. As he walked along the wet white sand he occasionally bent down to pick up a seashell. It was so soothing and peaceful here that he almost dreaded going back to the house when he saw Deborah Saunders walking from the other direction.

"Good morning!" he yelled. "Here I thought I was the virtuous early bird."

"Oh, Dr. Fleming," she said. "I cheated. I'm so excited about these plants I couldn't sleep. As soon as we can I want to move in and study the remaining plants in depth."

"Sit down," he said, pointing at one of the large pumice boulders recently washed up from Ahi. "Tell me why you're so excited."

"Aren't you?" she asked with surprise. "I thought that was why you came here, to be with us when we start testing the Ahi plants."

He smiled. "That's not what Dr. Evans thinks. He seems to believe I came down to horn in on his conversations with them."

"Oh, Ian." She dismissed him and the idea. "He's

convinced that we'll be talking to those plants by the end of the summer."

"It's strange, isn't it, Deborah? We always assume that we'll be talking to the plants, not that we might listen to them. It's as though we assume that they have nothing of interest to say to us."

He seemed so melancholy she was afraid that Ian Evans's words had hurt him. She tried to make up for them by telling him how happy she was that he had come out to see them.

"It's just an old man's curiosity, Deborah," he assured her. "I have great confidence in you and Ian."

"I know that; it's just that sometimes he talks as if he can't wait for you to retire."

"Don't let Ian bother you," he said gently. "He can be abrasive, but he's harmless."

"Oh, it's not Ian," she said. "I can handle him. It's those plants. Ian's right about the signals; I'm sure of it. They're coming from the plants and somehow they're influencing the others to produce enormous flowers and fruit."

"I should think you'd be pleased," Fleming chided. "These huge plants could be the answer to the world's food shortage."

Deborah stared down the white beach, so empty and quiet now. Farther ahead a large dead blowfish had been washed ashore. Two wild dogs sniffed around it, then moved away. She turned back to Dr. Fleming.

"There's more to those plants than the signals, doctor," she said. "I've examined the cuttings from Ahi and Nalowale and I've found something far more disturbing."

"Yes, go on," he encouraged.

"The Ahi plants have undergone substantial genetic changes," she said.

"Genetic?" His voice took on a note of concern. "What kind of changes, how substantial?"

She hesitated to say it, but she knew that Dr. Fleming was open-minded enough at least to consider her theory.

"When the four of us went to Ahi the other day, and found that little grove there in the middle of all that black-gray ash, all I was really thinking about was how beautiful it was."

"That's perfectly understandable, from the way you and Mr. Jenson described it, Deborah," Fleming tried to reassure her.

"It was only later, when we were sailing back to Nalowale and somebody remarked about the odd smell in the air that it came to me: the air in that little grove was loaded with carbon dioxide."

"Carbon dioxide?" Fleming repeated. "Did you mention this to the others?"

"No, I wanted to examine some cuttings before I could be sure, but now I am sure."

"Sure of what?"

"Those plants on Ahi have the ability to reverse the photosynthesis process, Dr. Fleming. Instead of producing oxygen, they apparently can also produce a high level of carbon dioxide in the air!"

"I see," he said gravely, recalling the description of the dead boy and girl they had found in the grove. "And you think that is what killed the two children?"

"Yes," she nodded.

"Say nothing about this for now, Deborah," he

ordered. "It may be nothing, so there's no reason to alarm the others." The idea of the plants producing carbon dioxide disturbed him more than he cared to admit. But it could all be for naught, he tried to tell himself. There was no reason to get alarmed until he had seen Ahi for himself and that would not be until after the defoliation. He stood up from the sand and brushed off his jeans. "Let's head back to the house, Deborah," he said. "It's almost time for the operation to begin."

Back at the house they found the others already huddled around Tom Jenson's radio. Although the operation was being directed from the *Defiant*, both helicopters would be in constant contact with Nalowale.

As they listened to the helicopters, Deborah could almost see the purple clouds of defoliant as they engulfed the island with only the brooding black cone of the volcano visible above it all.

Suddenly the voice of one of the helicopter pilots cracked across the radio.

"Air One to base, Air One to base." He had a Texas drawl and sounded very young. "This place is one purple haze, man. There isn't going to be a weed around here when this fades out."

"Air Two to base, Air Two to base," a second voice that could only be from Brooklyn came across. "Ahi is soaking in Myrozene. There isn't any way we missed an inch of this place."

"Air One," the voice came from the *Defiant*, "continue observation passes and report results. Air two, you may return to base."

For a few minutes there was silence in the tiny radio room as Deborah, Fleming, Evans, and Ryan bent over

Tom Jenson, eager to catch every word of Air One's observations, as he swept closer to the surface of Ahi Island. Suddenly the voice of Air One broke in.

"Air One to base," the Texas drawl had taken on an edge of excitement. "Sweep of Ahi Island complete. Results negative. Repeat, results negative."

"Oh, God," Deborah whispered as Dr. Fleming met her eyes. "The Myrozene had no effect at all."

Within two hours they were in protective suits, and on the launch, heading toward Ahi. As soon as the island came into view Deborah sensed that something was very wrong. There were more plants now, so many that they could make out the greenery from the launch.

"See, Dr. Fleming?" she said eagerly. "Over there on the left are the plants that sent the signals Ian tracked."

They disembarked hurriedly and waded in to shore.

"My God," Fleming whispered as he gazed about him. A clump of silverwood plants caught his eye and he stared at the tall stalks lined with gaudy purple and yellow flowers. These plants had no business here and the sight of them deeply disturbed him. By all the laws of nature they should not be growing on Ahi for several years after the violence had erupted. Now here they were in full flower just two months after the island had been turned into a fiery cauldron.

"This is nothing, Dr. Fleming," Tom Jenson was saying. "Wait until you see the grove." But even as they walked toward the grove where they had found the bodies of Malie and Makani, Tom realized it was unnecessary. The plants had spread and their way was lined with lush vegetation. There were more of the strange new plants with the triangular leaves; they seemed to be the most abundant.

"Believe me, Dr. Fleming," Deborah said. "None of this was here two days ago. There was just the grove and the clumps of the new plants on the other side of the island."

I believe you," Fleming said solemnly. "What concerns me is the way they reacted to the Myrozene. There's obviously going to be no question of a simple defoliation, I'm afraid."

"What's the alternative, Dr. Fleming?" Jenson asked.

"We're going to have to eliminate the plants entirely. We simply can't have them obstructing communications in this area."

"What are you saying?" Evans exploded. "What's a little static when you're talking about one of the greatest finds in history? Don't you understand? These plants are communicating with each other and these new ones," he gestured toward a bush with the odd new leaves, "are sending out some kind of signal that's making those plants on Nalowale grow twice their normal size. I'm sure of it."

Even Deborah was surprised at Dr. Fleming's radical decision. Surely a scientific discovery of this magnitude deserved more examination, and so she told him.

"Deborah, I understand your concern, and yours, too, Ian," he acknowledged. "But there can be no choice. These plants must be destroyed. And meanwhile, I think we have spent about as much time as we safely can here. I suggest we head back to Nalowale at once."

Deborah followed his lead gladly, while Evans, Ryan, and Jenson followed behind. Ryan took samples of the air.

"Man, that Myrozene sure does something to the air, don't it," he remarked.

"Yeah," Jenson said thoughtfully.

That night a disenchanted group met on the lanai of Jenson' house.

"I really don't feel in the mood for a luau," Ian Evans said, speaking for all of them, whether he realized it or not.

"I don't think any of us do," Jenson said. "But the Nalowalens don't get many guests and they're looking forward to seeing you.

"They'll never forgive me if I don't bring you."

"Where's Dr. Fleming?" Deborah asked as she joined the others. She had spend most of the last two days in a lab coat or a T-shirt and shorts, but tonight she had put on a pair of white linen trousers and a white halter that showed off her new tan. Her blond hair was loosely tied back with a white ribbon. She told herself she had taken special pains out of respect for the Nalowalens, but all the time she was taking her shower and dressing she had found to her surprise that she was thinking of Tom Jenson.

Three gloomy faces brightened only slightly when she sat down on the wide couch. Evans was pacing restlessly up and down and Ryan and Jenson had settled into the wicker armchairs.

"He said he had to take care of something on the launch," Jenson said. As soon as the words were out, the older scientist appeared.

"Well, it's done," he said gravely. "I've ordered that Ahi be fire-bombed tomorrow morning."

"What?" Ian Evans said angrily. "I thought it was

settled; I thought you were going to hold off a while!"

"No." Fleming shook his head. "We can't afford to delay. This is a serious matter, Ian. Far more serious than you realize."

"Would it have something to do with carbon dioxide, by any chance?" Jenson said casually.

The others looked at him, but his own eyes were on Fleming.

"The Oahu operator called in today with the results of the autopsy on Makani and Malie," he continued. "Carbon-dioxide narcosis. But I guess you already knew that, didn't you?"

Deborah stiffened. She should have realized from the way he acted on the island that he recognized something. But how? What did a layman know about carbon dioxide narcosis?

"Son of a gun," Mike Ryan exclaimed. "That's what was wrong with that air. I should have recognized that sour taste."

"Really, Mr. Jenson," Deborah said hastily, "carbon dioxide is hardly unusual around a volcano."

"But Ahi stopped erupting three months ago," he insisted. "Any carbon dioxide from that has long since diffused back into the atmosphere. Something on Ahi is producing enough carbon dioxide to kill a healthy young boy and girl, and I think you know what it is."

"Yes," she admitted. "It's the plants."

"Really, Deborah," Evans shouted, "that's a confidential matter. I can't believe you're discussing center business with an outsider.

"I'm hardly an outsider, Dr. Evans," Jenson said calmly. "I happen to live here and I have a right to know what's going on."

"Mr. Jenson is absolutely correct," Dr. Fleming added. "Go ahead, Deborah."

She turned back to Jenson and Ryan. "It's really quite simple. As you know, all green plants manufacture their own food through photosynthesis. They take carbon dioxide and water and with sunlight produce carbohydrates and oxygen. The oxygen goes back into the air, purified. That's why we depend on plants for our fresh air. They provide all the free oxygen in the atmosphere."

Ryan nodded. He vaguely remembered some of this from high school.

"Sometimes," Deborah continued, "in the absence of light or in the sections of the plant that aren't green, the plant reverses the process and makes water and carbon dioxide out of oxygen and organic matter. That's what's happening with the Ahi plants. They're producing carbon dioxide at an alarming rate."

"And that's what killed Makani and Malie?" Jenson asked. "The carbon dioxide the plants made?"

"I believe so." She nodded. "The closeness of the trees and bushes made that grove almost airtight. They must have felt groggy, the first symptom of carbon-dioxide narcosis, and instead of getting out of there they lay down. That was their fatal mistake."

"But those plants are green and there's plenty of sunlight on the island," Ryan protested. "Why did they produce the carbon dioxide?"

"There must have been a genetic change," Deborah answered. "I still don't understand exactly why they're doing it, but that is what they're doing."

"What about Nalowale, Dr. Saunders?" Jenson asked.

"Aren't we in danger of those plants producing carbon dioxide here?"

"No. Whatever it is in that volcano that's genetically altered the Ahi plants, there isn't a trace of genetic change in the plants on Nalowale."

"That's right," Evans added. He was reluctant to divulge information but anxious to make his own contribution clear. "My tests show that the plants on Nalowale are only responding to the signals from the Ahi plants. Those signals are what're causing their phenomenal growth. Somehow, the signals are acting as a stimulus."

"But because the Nalowale plants haven't altered genetically," Deborah added, "they can only receive messages, they can't transmit them."

"Kind of like the difference between a billion-dollar television station and a hundred-dollar TV," Ryan said.

Jenson said nothing. He was still not entirely satisfied. He poured another glass of coconut wine and leaned back in his chair. "If the plants are producing carbon dioxide, isn't that dangerous? They've already killed two kids."

"Don't be an alarmist, Jenson," Evans insisted. "We can learn from those plants. The fact that they're genetically advanced is what's important. The carbon-dioxide factor can be controlled. After the fire bombing tomorrow we'll move in on the remaining plants and work with them until we crack this thing."

"Just as simple as that," Jenson said dryly.

"That's right," Evans snapped. "As simple as that."

"But they're in the open air,doc," Ryan said to Dr. Fleming. "Won't the carbon dioxide just mix in with the rest of the air?"

"That's exactly the problem, Mike," he said. "You're all familiar with what is often call the greenhouse effect?"

Ryan shook his head. Jenson said nothing.

"I'll let Dr. Saunders explain." He nodded toward Deborah. "This is her area of expertise."

Deborah leaned forward in her chair and looked at the others earnestly. "The presence of carbon dioxide in the atmosphere keeps heat from radiating back into the atmosphere-- it works like glass in a hothouse," she began.

"So what are you telling us?" Ryan asked.

"It's simple, really," she continued patiently. "Carbon dioxide allows light rays from the sun to pass through it and to be absorbed by the surface of the earth. That absorption process generates heat and the carbon dioxide traps that heat in the atmosphere. A major increase in carbon dioxide could cause an increase in the temperature in the lower atmosphere--our atmosphere. Over a period of time that could result in flooding the coastal areas of the world."

Ryan whistled.

"You make it sound like a bunch of overgrown plants could alter the face the earth," Jenson said.

"Possibly," she answered. "A twenty-foot rise in the sea level could wipe out London and New York."

"Wow!" Ryan said. "That a lot of beach front property."

"It of course would depend on the rate of time in which it occurred. We have seen signs of this during the normal evolution of the earth. But if this current situation spreads and there is suddenly a rapid rise of temperature we could have real trouble, not only with water but also with a breathable environment."

"I still don't get it," Ryan interjected. "Volcanic eruptions aren't unusual, especially in the Pacific. What made this one so different? Why is the navy involved?"

Before his question could be answered they were interrupted by Keoni's voice as he entered the lanai.

"Hey, people." He grinned. "If you don't hurry you're going to miss the puaa kalua!"

Jenson laughed. "We wouldn't want to go to a luau and miss the roast pig, would we?" he teased, and then turned to the others. "Keoni's right. We'll have plenty of time to talk about Ahi tomorrow."

As they walked along the white beach they passed the outrigger canoes all strung now with the huge new gardenias and hibiscus. They looked like toy boats, almost hidden under the burden of the gaudy flowers. They moved on up to the village square where the air was warm and heavy with the fragrance of night-blooming cereus. Suddenly the flowers and trees began to rustle as a hot breeze passed through the village.

"It's the kona," Jenson explained. "The old Hawaiians call this dying weather."

"Very comforting," Ryan said dryly.

In the village itself every one of the New England-style houses was covered with flowers in cascades of color. Outside, on their small lawns, luxurious pink bombax trees and golden showers, rainbow showers, and flamboyant red royal Poinciana's competed for attention. Whatever the strange behavior of the plants, Deborah thought, it certainly gave a magnificent look to the island.

"Just who is this Kamehameha we're honoring tonight, Tom?" she asked.

"Kamehameha the Great," he corrected her. "He's the national hero of Hawaii. He united the islands under one rule at the turn of the nineteenth century."

"It sounds as if you identify with him a little," she teased.

Jenson smiled. "He was a tough old bird," he admitted. "Dined on a table service studded with the teeth of his enemies. They called him the Napoleon of the Pacific."

"Did he do anything besides wage war?" she asked.

"He managed to preserve Hawaiian culture in spite of the efforts of the missionaries and other 'civilizing' Westerners," Jenson said sharply. "His dynasty ended with Kamehameha V who died in 1872."

"I take it you don't think much of civilization?"

Jenson did not have a chance to reply because they had reached the village square. Flaming torches lighted it and most of the Nalowalens, from elderly grandmothers to little toddlers, were already there.

A pretty and very pregnant Nalowalen girl came up to them. She was wearing a bright red muumuu and lei of white gardenias around her neck. She smiled at Deborah.

"Ah, Tom." She giggled. "You have a sweetheart?"

Jenson looked embarrassed. "Dr. Saunders, meet Lani Maori," he said quickly. "The doctor is helping us clear up some problems, Lani."

Lani smiled, but she did not seem convinced. Then she frowned and deftly removed one of the plump white gardenias from her lei and placed it behind Deborah's ear. She stepped back and smiled with satisfaction.

"There, now you are properly dressed for a luau," she said.

"Thank you," Deborah said. For the first time she felt truly welcome on Nalowale.

"Come on," Keoni said impatiently. "You're going to miss something."

They moved toward the circle where the men were preparing the roast pork.

They were just in time to see them rubbing the insides of the skinned, scrubbed, and eviscerated pig with rock salt and soy sauce. Next, Keoni and several other boys placed the pig on a bed of chicken wire and the men lifted red-hot stones from the imu or underground oven with their bare hands. Deborah gasped as she saw them lift the glowing stones.

"Don't worry," Mike Ryan assured her. "Those guys don't feel a thing. They've done it a hundred times."

The men quickly stuffed the stones inside the pig, then tied its legs together, and wrapped it in the chicken wire. One of the older men raked the embers in the imu and the women, all dressed in brightly colored muumuus, lined the pit with banana leaves.

Next the men lowered the plump stuffed pig into the imu along with sweet potatoes and plantains. Once again Deborah was struck by the enormous size of the vegetables. Each sweet potato was the size of a large pumpkin and the plantains were each two feet long. The boys moved in to pile more banana leaves on top of the pig; the pile had to be thick enough to keep any steam from escaping. Quickly the women followed, covering the pit with a wet burlap blanket. The men then covered the blanket with heaping shovels full of red earth. Finally, a small giggling boy threw a bucket of water on the earth, sealing the imu.

"That was wonderful," Deborah said. "What happens next?"

"Well, it'll take four hours for the pig to steam," Jenson told them. "But there's a lot more happening."

They joined the rest of the group in forming a circle and into the middle stepped three young Nalowalen girls. They wore traditional grass skirts of long narrow tapa leaves and their long silky black hair covered their bare breasts. Each girl wore a crown of flowers, one red hibiscus, one white gardenia, and one yellow alamanda; and around her neck was a matching lei.

As an older woman in a bright yellow muumuu played the ukulele they began to hula, pantomiming the saga of King Kamehameha. To her surprise, Deborah understood most of the signals even without Keoni's simultaneous translation. With elegant gestures of their hands and arms the girls described Kamehameha's bravery and how he had united the five great Kona chiefs, ending warfare among the islands and uniting them under one king.

This was followed by a funny hula, all about the menehune, the little people who were supposed to have built many of the island lagoons. It told how fond they were of sweet potatoes and shrimp and Deborah found herself wondering what they would think of the new enormous sweet potatoes growing on Nalowale now.

While they watched the girls' dancing, the other Nalowalen women were laying various dishes on a long table near the imu. In no time at all it seemed that the men were lifting the savory pig out of the oven with great ceremony. Kuahiwi, befitting his status as village elder, sliced the pig with elaborate gestures and piled it on the plates. Then Deborah noticed something was missing.

"Where are the forks?" she asked.

Jenson began to laugh. "You eat with your fingers, Deborah, if you eat at all."

"Can you show me?"

Expertly Jenson began to pick up pieces of the hot pork and pop them into his mouth. Ignoring Ian Evans's glare, Deborah imitated the gesture. To her surprise the roast pig was rich and delicious.

"What about all that?" she pointed at the table.

"Oh, you've got to have poi," Jenson insisted, dropping a

purple-brown lump on her plate.

"Don't miss the opihi," Mike Ryan warned, adding a bit of black shellfish. "It's the caviar of Hawaii."

"No, you've got to have the laulaus," Dr. Fleming said firmly, adding what looked vaguely like stuffed cabbage

Deborah looked down at the plate heaped with strange delicacies and did not know whether to laugh or cry. She had vaguely heard of poi and seen the word in crossword puzzles, but the rest was totally alien.

"Look, guys," she finally said, "I'll try anything, but I've got to know what it is." Jenson explained that poi was the staple of Hawaii and was made from pounding taro root. She ate it with her fingers, just like the pork.

"It's good," she said with surprise.

"And it's loaded with vitamin B," Dr. Fleming, ever the scientist, assured her. The opihi tasted like a salty little clam and the laulaus turned out to be ti leaves wrapped around bits of pork, butterfish, and tender green vegetable. It even tasted a little like stuffed cabbage.

They drank a punch from broken coconut shells as the village girls with crowns of gardenias and orchids in their hair walked through the group sprinkling bits of dried seaweed, rock salt, and chopped roasted kukui nuts on their plates.

As evening fell some of the Nalowalens sat around the fire and played ukuleles and sang until the older party-goers began to disappear. More ukuleles appeared and Deborah and the others joined in singing traditional Hawaiian songs. Gradually, though, the crowd thinned. Dr. Fleming yawned and announced that he was turning in. Ryan and Evans joined him.

"I hate to leave now," Deborah sighed as she rose to go. "It's so wonderful, I hate to miss anything."

"Then don't leave," Jenson said. "Stay with me."

"Thank you," she said, mildly surprised. She sat down beside him as the others left and they listened to three of the men sing about still more of the adventures of the great Kamehameha. Eventually, though, even they ran out of tales and soon only a handful of revelers was left.

"I suppose we'd best be going," Jenson said casually. "Would you like to walk back along the beach? It's beautiful at this time of night."

"Yes, I'd like that," she said and following Jenson she made her way gingerly in the darkness until they arrived at the beach. There, in spite of the hour, the reflection of the full moon on the white sands bathed the beach in a warm golden light.

"Would you like to see my favorite part of the

island?" he said softly.

"Yes." She smiled, unsure what was to come.

He took her hand and together they waded around a high pile of lava rocks at the end of the beach. On the other side was a passageway in the hard black rock so narrow that they had to pass through single file, but at the other end was another world.

"Oh, it's lovely," she gasped. Inside was a lagoon, fed by the Pacific but warm and tranquil as though it were a million miles away from the ocean instead of only a few feet.

Four tall flamingos waded in the shallow pool while varicolored fish darted about the water. Huge pink and yellow orchids were flourishing among the lava rocks.

"Sit down," he said and they both sat down on a rock, their feet hanging in the warm water of the pool.

"Hawaii is forever surprising me," she said. "Even this small island has so much, so many beautiful places, so unspoiled."

"Not for long," he said, staring at the white flower in her hair. "You should always wear flowers in your hair."

"Thank you," she said. "I guess if I lived here I could."

"It's not a bad life," he observed. "I always thought I would spend the rest of my life here."

"And now, Mr. Jenson?"

"Please," he said, taking her hand and drawing her toward him. "Call me Tom."

"And I'm Deborah," she whispered as she responded to his kiss in a way that totally surprised her.

But the peacefulness of the moment was suddenly broken by shouts.

"Tom! Tom!" Keoni's voice called from the other side of the lagoon. "Come quick and bring the doctor."

Deborah looked at Tom. "Does he mean me?"

"There's only one way to find out," he said, standing up and helping her to her feet. They hurried out of the lagoon and onto the beach. Keoni was waiting for them, jumping up and down nervously. With him were two Nalowalen women Deborah recognized from the luau. But their faces were clouded now and they were solemn and obviously nervous.

"Come quick, Dr. Saunders," one of the women said. "Lani has gone into labor. She's having big trouble."

Deborah exchanged glances with Tom; his face was solemn but inscrutable. "Excuse me," she told Keoni and the women as she pulled him aside.

Tom," she whispered. "They think I'm a medical doctor! What should I do?"

"You can't do anything until you see what the trouble is," he answered. "Go on, there must be something you can do when you get there."

"All right," she agreed. "But please come with me. I need your support." Then she turned back to the women. "Take me to Lani."

Jenson smiled to himself as he and Keoni followed the three women back to the Maori house. The way she could so easily switch from competent professional to sensitive woman, and then back again, appealed to him.

As they walked in the darkness the two women explained the situation to Deborah. Lani Maori was seven months pregnant with her first child. Nothing had happened to alarm them; then, suddenly, after the luau, she had gone into premature labor. That had been hours ago and nothing was happening. The girl was in great pain.

When they arrived at the house it was ablaze with light and they hurried inside, past a cluster of relatives whispering in the living room, and on to the rear bedroom.

Lani lay on a large old-fashioned brass bed. Her skin was ashen and her long black hair was matted with perspiration. Her mother, a tall stately woman, still wearing the green flowered muumuu she had on at the luau, leaned over to wipe her face with a wet cloth. When she touched her the girl smiled and took her hand. Deborah moved quickly to the other side of the bed and took up Lani's slender wrist. Her pulse was beating wildly. Suddenly, the girl screamed.

"It's coming," she moaned, but the rest of her words were in Hawaiian, which Deborah did not understand. The girl was right, the baby was coming. One of the Nalowalen women had brought a small basin of warm water and it stood close by. The only sound in the room were Lani's screams.

Then suddenly it was over as, in a convulsive movement, her body gave up the child. After the cord had been tied and cut Deborah took the baby and brought it to the basin.

Later she would realize that she knew something was wrong the minute she took the tiny body in her arms. Since she had never held a newborn child before she was not positive until she began gently to rinse away the blood.

She left Lani's mother alone; the woman was too busy with her daughter to notice anything else. Then she turned back to the baby.

As the blood turned the basin red, the tiny newborn was revealed to have a slight bluish color around the mouth and the body was limp. She slapped the baby gently on the bottom, but no sound came. Then she watched the chest area anxiously but there was no sign of movement. “Tom,” she called running to the door.

He entered quickly and at a glance took in the situation. Gently he took the child in his arms and, placing his mouth over the tiny nose and mouth, he blew quick puffs of air into it. Simultaneously he placed two fingers on the infant’s chest and applied compressions. For what seemed like an eternity there was no response.

Suddenly Lani screamed, a long shrill scream of pain and desolation.

Deborah looked on in alarm and switched her gaze between Jenson and Lani, and then to everyone’s delight the unmistakable cry of the baby filled the room.

Hastily Tom wrapped the tiny body in a soft blanket and the placed the now pink-cheeked little girl in her mother’s arms.

Deborah turned quickly and, as her eyes met the mother's, she knew that Lani Maori would be fine.

Lani's young husband held her hand as they waited for the helicopter that would take them and the baby to Ohau for observation. He was overjoyed that everything had worked out so well and the smile on Lani’s face as she cuddled the baby girl to her breast spoke volumes.

Tom and Deborah drove back in silence, but as they entered the quiet house Tom put his hand on Deborah’s arm and asked, “How are you doing?”

“I was so scared back there,” she sighed.

"Look, Deborah," he said firmly. "It was touch and go, but everything turned out fine and you were great."

"Thank you," she said, but tears filled her eyes even as she spoke. "It's over," he said. "Now get a good night's sleep and we'll worry about other problems tomorrow."

-Nine-

At dawn, Dr. Fleming, wearing a festive yellow and red aloha shirt was waiting on the beach for the navy helicopter to take him on the firebombing mission. To his surprise, young Keoni was already preparing his trimaran, still draped with flowers, for a morning's fishing. He greeted him, and Keoni told him the news about Lani Maori.

"I want to get a head start on the fish today," the boy said. "Lately something's been getting to them before we do."

"Oh, really?" The older man perked up. "What's that?"

The boy shrugged. "I don't know, Dr. Fleming. Maybe that interference Tom is always talking about."

"Could you show me some of these fish?" Fleming asked.

"Sure, they're floating all around the reef. I'll bring some back for you." He looked up at the sky suddenly. "I think your helicopter's here, doctor."

The air was filled with the clatter of rotating blades as the white helicopter descended. The pilot leaned out and grinned at the older man and the small boy.

"Which one of you is Dr. Fleming?" he asked in the

now familiar Texas drawl.

Keoni pointed at the scientist. "This is your man," he yelled above the sound of the rotors. "So long, doctor."

The doctor stepped into the helicopter and it immediately ascended into the air as Keoni waved furiously on the ground below.

"I'm Cody Stanton," the young pilot said. "Better known as Air One."

"How do you do, Cody," Fleming said politely.

"I understand that the Myrozene had no effect at all," the pilot continued. "So this time we're going in with napalm."

"That's right," Fleming acknowledged. "We're experimenting with new methods of eliminating underbrush. This island's uninhabited so it's the perfect place to test."

That was a good enough explanation for Cody. They had passed over the blue Pacific and were now approaching Ahi Island.

"Captain Fraser thought you'd want a front-row seat," he said. "So you can stay with me when we make the drop instead of waiting on the *Defiant*."

"Excellent," Fleming agreed.

"Air Two and the other choppers are waiting for us over Ahi right now," he added. "Look, there they are."

Fleming could see the other white helicopter circling in the air. Below, the island was more lushly overgrown than ever. The trees and vines now almost obscured the specter of the black lava cone of the volcano.

The voice of Captain Fraser came across the helicopter radio. "Air One, come in, Air One."

Cody took up the mike. "This is Air One. Go ahead."

"Are you ready to begin your drop?"

"Ready."

"Air Two, come in, Air Two."

The voice of Brooklyn responded. "This is Air Two; go ahead.

"Are you ready to begin the drop?"

"Ready."

"Prepare to drop, Air Two."

"Go," Fraser ordered.

Each group of helicopters dropped a series of thin-skinned bombs that ruptured as they hit lava rocks, trees, and plants, igniting and spilling flaming liquid everywhere.

"This mixture of gasoline and heavier petroleum oil and other pyrotechnic chemicals will burn at 1800 degrees Fahrenheit. Those flames will stick to the plants until they're completely burned out," Stanton told Fleming as they watched the pyrotechnics.

Below them the sky was bright with orange flames, a brilliant burning fiery mass. Only the ominous black top of the volcano was visible above the wall of flames. Stanton maneuvered the chopper around the island for thirty minutes. There was no doubt that between them the two helicopter groups had bathed every inch of Ahi in incredible heat and flames.

Cody picked up the mike again to communicate with the *Defiant*.

"Air One to base," he drawled.

"Go ahead, Air One," the *Defiant* operator answered.

"We've completed the run and the island is engulfed in smoke and flame. Air Two will proceed to begin low-level inspection, other units returning to carrier."

"Roger, Air One. Base standing by."

Fleming watched with interest as the helicopter descended. Suddenly the voice of Air Two became excited.

"The fires are going out all over the island!" he yelled.

"Did he say going out?" Fleming shouted and then stopped. He was anxious not to give the pilot the impression that this was anything but a routine mission.

"That's affirmative, sir," Stanton replied,

"Air Two now dropping to two hundred fifty feet to get a closer look."

"Go ahead, Air Two," the voice of the *Defiant* acknowledged.

"I am now 250 feet over Ahi Island; there are burned patches on the ground and lots of smoke, but no fire." The voice of Brooklyn laughed nervously and then there was silence.

"Air Two, I'm losing you," the voice of the *Defiant* came back after a few minutes. "It's that damned interference again."

"Air Two to base," the voice came back suddenly. "I'm in trouble. My radio's breaking up and my instruments aren't functioning." The aircraft began to vibrate violently. Brooklyn became disoriented and overcome by a wave of nausea, as he desperately fought to control the aircraft.

Cody, picked up the mike. "Air Two, this is Air One; can you read me?" They could just make out the other helicopter in the billowing black smoke. If he could follow them he would not need the instruments.

But Brooklyn could not hear a thing. "Air Two to base," he called plaintively. "If you read me, I repeat, chopper out of control, instruments don't respond, sudden heavy turbulence. Base, I..."

"Oh, my God!" Cody shouted as they watched Air Two disappear into the cloud of smoke and flame that engulfed the island.

Fleming gripped the sides of his seat as Air One began to shake. The even rhythm of the rotors above them suddenly became erratic. He looked over at Stanton whose brow was covered with sweat. "Climb, he ordered. Climb now!" Below them the smoke of the extinguished firebombs was thick and black. He could almost feel the heat from their altitude of two hundred feet.

The *Defiant* operator began urgently to signal them. "Air One, base to Air One, come in Air One!"

Stanton turned to Dr. Fleming, all his torment visible in his young face. "There's nothing. I've lost all contact. It's like we're being jammed and we're still losing altitude." He turned back to the mike. "Air One to base, Air One to base."

Another, more authoritative voice came over the waves. "Air One, this is Captain Fraser. What is your situation?"

"This is Air One. Chopper damaged. I'm having difficulty maintaining altitude. Air Two is gone."

Then as suddenly as it began the trouble cleared. "Air One to base. We've got it under control. Will be making an emergency landing, ETA fifteen minutes."

Fleming let out a sigh of relief as Air One touched down on the *Defiant*. Captain Fraser was waiting for them and so were other members of the crew. They were obviously disturbed at the loss of the young pilot and the unexplained destruction of a high tech helicopter.

"Are you okay, son?" Fraser asked Stanton.

"I am now, sir, but for a while there I was not sure we would make it. My head hurt and I thought I was going to lose my lunch."

"I believe that was caused by exposure to a strong subsonic wave, son," replied Fleming, "the same type that has been causing all the interference in this area."

Sure that the young pilot was all right, Fraser turned to Fleming. "What happened out there, doctor? First a routine defoliation fails, and now we've lost a man. Something jammed our communications and brought down our chopper."

"I'm afraid I can't tell you any more than that," Fleming said firmly.

"Well, we'll be sending you back to Nalowale in a few minutes, Dr. Fleming," Fraser said. "And then we'll move in to see what's left of poor Lopez and Air Two."

"That will be impossible, captain," Fleming said.

"I beg your pardon," Fraser said. "I'm in command of this ship."

"Yes, Captain Fraser," Fleming acknowledged. "But if you'll check with Admiral Wilson at Pearl you'll find that I have priority. And, as of now, I'm declaring Ahi Island off limits to all but authorized personnel."

"You're telling me I can't go in and retrieve the body of one of my men?" Fraser's tone was disbelieving

"That's exactly what I'm telling you, captain," Fleming nodded. "All I can tell you is that you saw what just happened to one of your men, I'm sure you don't want to see a repeat performance."

"I'll check with Admiral Wilson immediately," Fraser

said coldly. “Meanwhile, I think it's best to get you back to Nalowale immediately. I don't want you on my ship.”

“I understand,” Fleming nodded sadly.

The Defiant crewman took him back to Nalowale in silence and Fleming hardly blamed him. He, too, had heard the anguished cries of the young pilot of Air Two as he went down. But he did not understand the real implications of the renewed interference. No, that was a secret that Fleming could only share with his four associates waiting on Nalowale.

The white helicopter landed on the beach and took off immediately. As soon as the sound of the rotors had faded, he told them what had happened over Ahi.

“We saw the chopper go down,” Ryan said. “I was watching the operation with my binoculars and suddenly the thing exploded. For a minute we thought it was you.”

Fleming shook his head. He suddenly felt very tired. This was combat and combat was a young man's business. He was not a young man anymore.

“Have you noticed how much the interference has increased?” he asked as they walked back to Jenson' house. “It's as if the plants are taunting us, gloating over their superiority.”

“How could they do something like this?” Ian Evans asked. He was the only one who seemed to be relishing the combat.

“If I’m not mistaken, Ian,” Fleming answered. “That helicopter was destroyed by a very high form of subsonic wave which literally tore it apart. The plants emitted the carbon dioxide that smothered the fires.”

“Which means that they can control and modulate those frequencies, and increase the carbon-dioxide emissions whenever they want," Evans replied.

"Yes, Ian," Fleming said with concern. "It seems that so far all our efforts to control or destroy the Ahi plants have only succeeded in increasing their activities."

That night Mike Ryan served a dinner of broiled grouper and sweet potatoes. Once, he noted, he would have needed one potato for each person, but with the huge new growth on Nalowale, one sweet potato was enough for the five of them.

They seemed to be consciously avoiding talking about Ahi, but each subject only led back to the one that was on all their minds. Finally Jenson spoke for them all.

"Dr. Fleming, it seems that the Ahi plants are a lot more developed than any of us suspected," he said. "Don't you think it's about time you told us everything?"

"What do you mean?" the older man said softly.

"Come on, Dr. Fleming," Jenson said this time with more of an edge in his voice. "I know something about biology and no simple volcano could cause the genetic changes we've seen. And a lot of hot lava doesn't make a homicidal plant."

Deborah gasped. So he had shared her suspicions. Somehow these strange creatures were connected somehow to the center. And now Tom was right. She had been so wrapped up in her own work and loyalty to Dr. Fleming that she had refused to face the truth. Dr. Fleming did know more than he was telling. He was hiding something.

She looked at him and Fleming could read the disappointment in her face.

He hesitated and then looked squarely at Jenson. "You're right, Mr. Jenson. You all have a right to know everything that's going on."

"What are you talking about?" Ian Evans demanded.

"Just what is going on, Dr. Fleming?" Jenson asked.

"Ahi has been used as a test area for decades. It is not your average volcanic island and the botanical growth on the island is far from your normal plant life," Fleming explained.

"What?" Jenson shouted so loudly that the flowers around the lanai seemed to shake. "I don't like the sound of that."

The doctor continued reluctantly, but he had agreed to tell them the truth and it was going to be the whole truth. "Kaolani Center was founded in 1965 as a research institute initially to support our space program, primarily the lunar missions conducted by Apollo. The Ahi site was officially closed down in 1975 three years after the end of the Apollo project."

"I don't remember any tests being conducted in this area of the Pacific," Ryan said shaking his head slowly.

"You're right, Mr. Ryan. Since everything connected with the project was top secret, we chose an area where there was little or no chance of attracting attention."

He paused and looked at the faces around the table to see how the others were taking this revelation. Jenson looked annoyed, Ryan merely shocked. Deborah and Ian were both equally surprised. But where Deborah looked concerned and supportive, Ian actually seemed to be enjoying Fleming's discomfort.

"I'll be damned." Ryan whistled, pouring himself another glass of wine, he continued, "You mentioned NASA and the Apollo Project. What's the connection?"

"As you know, during the course of the Apollo

program literally hundreds of pound of rocks and soil samples were brought back for analysis. What you don't know is that during a routine spectroscopic analysis it was discovered that what was initially thought to be dead volcanic soil contained golf ball- size seed pods, possibly millions of years old."

"Seed pods!" Deborah exclaimed. "That's incredible."

"Our feeling exactly," Fleming continued. "The pods were subjected to dozens of tests. Then, quite by accident, we made an amazing discovery. We irradiated some of the pods to observe the effect on the seeds and to our dismay the pods opened and released seeds into the soil. Within hours seedling began to appear. After a few days they withered and died."

Deborah could no longer contain herself. "How could you keep this a secret?" she blurted. We were looking for microbes and you had a new living species."

"The truth is we didn't know for sure what we had and we're still not sure. We felt that if we could place the pods in a similar soil environment we might make a breakthrough. The volcanic ash and soil on Ahi closely resembled the moon's surface. Under the guise of geological observations we placed some of pods on the island. We then placed small samples of radioactive isotopes around the plants to continue the irradiation process.

"We selected Ahi because it was so remote, and far from the major shipping lanes," he went on. "Except for a few samples kept in the lab for observation the remaining soil samples containing the pods were hermetically sealed in three specially designed canisters and placed into the crater of the volcano"

"You dropped canisters filled with a possible new alien life form into a potential cauldron?" Jenson's voice was disbelieving.

"We gave it a lot of thought, Mr. Jenson, and all indications at the time told us that it would be hundreds of years before the volcano erupted again, if ever."

"Boy," Jenson said, "and I thought cities were scary."

"That was in 1972," Fleming continued. "We watched for three years and nothing happened. We sealed the rest of the samples and over the years the project was forgotten. That is, until now."

"Doctor, are you telling us that you believe that an alien plant life is the cause of all of these problems?" Jenson asked incredulously.

"More precisely, Mr. Jenson, I believe that we have an alien life which strongly resembles a botanical life form."

"Oh, that makes me feel much better," Jenson said dubiously,and continued. "So if you're right, what happened to trigger this incredible situation?"

"Several months ago we detected a large thermal vent developing below Ahi Island."

"A what?" Ryan asked.

"Sorry," Fleming said. "Let me explain. A thermal vent occurs when pressure building near the floor of the ocean creates an opening. Sort of an underwater smoke stack, if you will. They are heated by boiling magma which forces large amounts of super- heated water to the surface. The force of these phenomena is incredible and the water temperature can exceed 650F. I can only guess, but I suspect that the recent quake caused the vent to form and it in turn caused the unexpected eruption of the volcano. When the lava heated up it spilled out covering the island and mixing with the radioactive material placed around the pods and in the crater. In some way, I'm sure it affected the Ahi plants."

Jenson tried to make sense of this startling bit of news. "So, the Kaolani Center had been involved with Ahi Island for years. How does the center get its funding, Doctor?"

"None of your business," Ian Evans snapped, but Fleming waved his hand in a dismissive gesture.

"The center is funded by the Kaolani Foundation, Mr. Jenson, and in answer to your next question, yes, we receive most of our money from the Department of Defense."

"So you're really just a front, aren't you?"

"I wouldn't go that far, Mr. Jenson," Fleming said slowly, but Deborah Saunders interrupted. She could not take watching Jenson berate him anymore.

"The Kaolani Center does important work in Hawaii, Tom, and its much more than a front."

"But you've gone to some lengths to hide the fact that you're a government operation, haven't you?" Tom said as he turned back to Dr. Fleming. "Just one more question, sir. Whom do you report to in Washington?"

Fleming sighed; Ian Evans looked angry; Deborah Saunders seemed concerned. Mike Ryan merely stared, still trying to digest this latest news.

"I report to the president," Dr. Fleming said dryly. "It began with Mr. Johnson in the 1960's and succeeding presidents have inherited the center and its director."

Silence reigned at the table until Dr. Fleming spoke

again. "Let me assure you, Mr. Jenson, that this was never meant to be a military operation. The Kaolani Center was and is a research organization dedicated to investigating the causes and effects of all geological and volcanic events. The last thing we wanted to do was totally destroy these plants. That's why we tried defoliation in the first place. We merely wanted to slow down the process that seems to be unfolding and buy some time to observe them. If things continue as they have during the last several months life, as we know it, could be considerably altered."

"What I'd like to know" interrupted Mike Ryan, is where the hell those thing came from in the first place. I don't ever remember reading that the moon was a lush tropical paradise."

"You're right, Mike, we don't think they originated there either. Something else that was never reported was that, in addition to finding the pods, the Apollo crew unearthed the wreckage of what they believe to be a spacecraft of unknown origin. It also appears to have been there for some time, perhaps centuries.

"Boy it just keeps getting better," Ryan said finishing the last of his wine.

"Doctor Fleming, do we have any idea where they may have originated?"

"I'm afraid not, Deborah," he replied. Plant life even as we know it has been evolving for hundreds of millions of years as have many others including microscopic life such as bacteria. Some of the oldest fossils of living creatures appear to be a microscopic form of vegetation. Some varieties of algae may have originated over 2 billion years ago. Even early species of flowering plants may date back close to 100 million years.

"What Dr. Fleming is trying to tell you," Ian Evans said curtly, "is that whatever these things are they could precede us by billions of years, and they have evolved many times to continue their species. They want to survive and they will at any cost, unless we can halt the process."

"I propose a toast," Ryan announced, raising his glass of coconut wine. "To victory."

"But over what?" Jenson asked. All five glasses clinked together. Outside the darkness closed in around them.

-Ten-

The next morning they took the launch to Ahi. As they cut through the blue surf and the island came into view, Deborah was shocked to see that it was more lushly overgrown than ever. Only the brooding black crater of the volcano served to remind them that this had once been a dead island.

But there was something more; a sensation that they were not alone, that something was watching their every move. “I wonder if they know who we are,” she whispered as they disembarked and waded toward the shore. She noticed the corpses of several dead fish floating in the shallow water. “Look at these, Dr. Fleming,” she said. “What do you make of them?”

“Young Keoni mentioned yesterday that a lot of fish were turning up dead,” Fleming said gravely. Then he turned to Evans. “I think you'd better have a look at some of them when we get back, Ian. We should know what killed them.”

“You don't think they're connected to the plants, do you, doc?” Ryan asked.

“I don’t know, Mike,” he said. “But I think we should look into anything unusual.” When they reached the shore Jenson looked around cautiously. “I suggest we stick together this time," he said. "We don't know what's happened here since our last visit."

Slowly, the small band began to move toward the lush forest. Ryan was in the lead, monitoring his frequency scanner. Deborah was closely watching the small digital C02 sensor strapped to her wrist. "I would have thought that the radiation levels would have been higher, in light of what has occurred here, doctor."

"Yes I've been wondering about that myself. I believe that whatever these things are they are absorbing much of the radiation. If not for that I don't believe we would be able to remain here very long. Even in protected suits."

"Hey, doc, look at this," Ryan called. "The read-out fluctuates as I move toward different plants."

"Different reactions are not really unexpected," Fleming said calmly. "It just strengthens my theory that some of the species are stronger and more advanced than others. If we can stop the leaders, the rest will be neutralized."

They moved gingerly among the charred wreckage of Air Two. Already vines and grass were beginning to cover it. After examining the craft Fleming said, "Collect some samples of the metal. I want it analyzed. We will take the remains of the pilot back with us for proper burial."

They cautiously approached the grove where they had found the bodies of Makani and Malie. The growth of the palm trees seemed even more luxuriant, and several rainbow shower trees had joined the huge pink bombax. Ryan moved his measuring equipment closer to an odd vine-like object with triangular leaves.

“This may be what we're looking for,” said Dr. Fleming. “The signal from this grove seems to be the strongest. What are the radiation readings, Dr. Saunders?”

“They've increased, Dr. Fleming,” Deborah answered. “But they're still in the safety zone.”

Fleming stared at the strange form. “I'll have to bring back some samples to analyze in the lab.”

“I'll cut a piece for you,” Jenson offered. He began to move toward the vine.

“Be careful, Mr. Jenson,” the older scientist warned. “We don't want to alarm them.”

Jenson pulled out his knife and began to cut a thin branch. Suddenly the huge plant began to shake. The triangular leaves caught his hand and he could not pull free. He struggled as the others watched in horror until finally the plant creature released him and he fell back to the ground.

Deborah rushed toward him. “Tom, are you all right?” She knelt down beside him and examined his hand

Jenson was slightly dazed and stared at his hand as she held it. There was a three-inch gash, not very deep but painful. Then he stood up and looked at Fleming.

“That thing knew what it was doing, didn't it, Dr. Fleming?”

“I think you're the best judge of that, Mr. Jenson.”

“It did,” he said firmly. His hand was beginning to swell. It felt as if it had been caught in a door.

Ryan looked around nervously while the others were talking. The plants had begun to stir and the monitoring equipment was responding. Then the signals faded again.

Whatever they were talking about was over.

"I think we'd better quit while we're ahead," Ryan announced. "That was too close for comfort."

"No," Jenson said. "We're here and we're going to get samples. Mike, you stay with me. The rest of you guys hit the beach we will work on this baby."

They were reluctant to leave them alone with the threatening plant, but they insisted. They waited until they were gone; then Jenson turned back to study the entity with the odd-shaped leaves. The air was steamy and he could almost taste the sour flavor of the carbon dioxide. They would have to move fast before they started to feel the effects.

It all looked so ordinary. That was what bothered him the most. If he had not seen the way the equipment reacted he would never have believed there was anything unusual about it. But the way the plant had gripped him proved there was something wrong. That plant had wanted to hurt him. It knew what it was doing.

It knew what it was doing.

Maybe Fleming was wrong. Maybe the Ahi plants were working on more than instinct. He edged closer to the plant. The grove was silent, no leaves rustled. But they were watching him, he was sure of it.

Slowly, he took his knife in his left hand and raised it over the plant and then swiftly he brought it down. As he expected, the plant went for it, swinging its branches boldly toward his left hand. Simultaneously, he pulled back his left hand while breaking off a piece with his right hand. He could almost hear the plant's cry of pain.

The leaves on the nearby plants began to rustle furiously as he leaped away from the odd plant. But it was too late; he had what he wanted.

“I fooled you, didn't I?” He began to laugh as he waved the leafy branch. “You've still got a lot to learn.” Then he turned and ran toward the waiting boat.

“You got it!” Deborah yelled when she saw him.

“Yes, ma'am, but I wouldn't want to meet that plant again.” He climbed into the boat and Ryan started up the engine. “Let's get out of here.”

As they were speeding back to Nalowale, Deborah showed Jenson some of the charred cuttings she had picked up on Ahi.

“The napalm wasn't totally ineffective; it got a few of the weaker plants,” she said. “I'll examine these in the lab when we get back to Nalowale.”

“Why bother with the losers?” Jenson asked.

“You'd be surprised, Tom. We can learn a lot from them. What we have on Ahi is an accelerated evolution. Some of these losers that lived only a few weeks on Ahi could go on for centuries in the world as we know it.”

He grinned at her and absent-mindedly stroked his beard. “You're the first person, Deborah, to make science sound interesting to me.”

She smiled. “I never thanked you for taking that branch from the Ahi plant, Tom. You were very brave.”

“Brave?” He shook his head. “It was pure male pride. I just couldn't stand having him beat me.”

“Suppose the plant's a female?” she asked with a smile.

“Even worse.” He laughed and in spite of herself she joined him.

“The world seems very small, now, doesn't it?” she said as Dr. Fleming joined them on the bow. “We're a very insignificant part of it."

"What happens here may determine how much longer it remains our world," Dr. Fleming said.

"Do you really believe that the Ahi botanical life forms could threaten the human race, Dr. Fleming?" Jenson asked.

"Yes, I do."

"But how? We still have the ability to reason and we have mobility and an arsenal of weapons. How long could they survive against all that?"

"The question is how long we can survive, Tom." The doctor slowly shook his head. "We take for granted the fact that plants are essential for maintaining our ecosystem, for producing all our free oxygen. "Without oxygen we would lose our ability to reason and all our mobility and weapons would be useless." He stared out at the clear blue water and then turned back to Jenson and Deborah.

"Have you noticed any build-up in the seaweed around here lately?"

Yes," Jenson acknowledged. "It has been awful thick for this time of year."

"I've noticed quite a bit washed up on the beaches of Nalowale," Deborah added. "Dr. Fleming, do you think this has spread to the sea?"

"I'm not sure, Deborah, and I don't want to be an alarmist," the doctor said quietly. "But I think you had better have a look at some of it in the lab as well."

As they stood on the bow, silently deliberating this new potential challenge, another corpse of a beautiful silvery marlin floated by, followed by a clump of green seaweed. No one bothered to mention that it was a larger clump than they had ever seen before.

As soon as they were back on the island, the three scientists entered the lab area to examine the evidence they had picked up on Ahi while Jenson and Ryan returned to the house.

The lab was small but almost as well equipped as the lab at Kaolani. There were two long tables; Deborah worked at one and Evans at the other. Both tables were lined with racks of test tubes, reagents, and chemicals. They were equipped with light microscopes; phase, polarizing, and interference microscopes; a recording spectrophotometer, and a radioisotope counter. At the end of the cabin was an electron microscope capable of magnifying hundreds of times more than a light microscope through a beam of electrons.

All three had donned their lab coats and Deborah and Evans were both deeply absorbed in their experiments, Deborah on the plants and Evans on the fish. Fleming moved between them, offering suggestions and occasionally pitching in.

"There must be a weak spot," Deborah insisted over and over. Her blond hair was pulled back in a tight topknot and stray strands kept escaping, but she was too distracted to notice. "We must find it before it's too late."

Deborah was checking the results of exposing the plants to ultraviolet light. Some research had indicated that plant cells communicated by emitting ultraviolet rays and it had been useful in inducing mutations. She sighed with impatience as she recorded the results of her own experiment in the log. Just as she had expected, the signals had increased in strength and frequency, cellular activity had increased, and the exchange of electromagnetic energy had accelerated. When she withdrew the ultraviolet light they became somewhat dormant but still far more resistant than normal plants.

"Nothing here, Dr. Fleming," she said unhappily.

"Don't be discouraged, Deborah," he said. "The plants' resistance isn't that much of a surprise."

"It isn't?"

"No, many plants are adapted to regular fires, those *OHIA LEHUA* trees can be almost completely buried by red-hot cinders in a volcanic eruption and they'll still sprout." He shook his head at the wonder of it all. In spite of their troubles he still had a lot of admiration for the achievements of the Ahi life forms. "They'll even form new roots immediately in the new warm ash."

"It's as though they have acquired all the tenaciousness of every breed," Deborah said.

"I'm afraid that's exactly what we're up against," Fleming replied. "They skipped hundreds of years of genetic trial and error to produce a species that seems to be immune to everything we know."

"So far we've tried chemicals and heat. I'd like to see them under a sodium light," she said, "to see how they react to cold."

Together they prepared the sodium vapor lamps and placed the tagged samples under the yellow glow.

"Look at the way they're shaking already, doctor," she said with excitement.

"You think that's news?" Evans said as he completed his own test. "Your hunch about those fish, was right, Dr. Fleming. They all died of carbon-dioxide narcosis.

Deborah turned to Dr. Fleming. "So it's spread to the sea, hasn't it?"

"It may have, Deborah," he said cautiously. "But so far I don't think the seaweed shows much serious genetic change. It's still at the same developmental level as the plants here on Nalowale."

"Which means that they're under the control of the Ahi plants," Evans added. "Damn it, Dr. Fleming,we've got to communicate with them."

"I know, I know," the older scientist agreed. "Let's see what's happening under the sodium light."

Evans sighed and followed the two of them back to the lab table.

"Oh, Dr. Fleming," Deborah shouted when she saw the plants. "I think we may have gotten a break; they are vulnerable to the sodium light."

"Excellent," the doctor agreed. "Continue to hit them with the vapor and I'll check the cell structure."

He took one of the tagged samples, scraped off a tiny bit, and prepared a slide. Then he examined the slide under the microscope. The bombardment of cold had affected the cellular activity.

"I think this is the Achilles' heel we've been looking for, Deborah," he said as he stepped aside to let Ian look through the microscope.

"I can see it happened, Dr. Fleming," Evans said. "But why?"

"First, let's not be too optimistic," he cautioned. "Freezing the cells hasn't destroyed the Ahi plants any more than the defoliant or fire-bombing did. But it does seem to have substantially weakened them."

"At least it's something, doctor," Deborah encouraged him.

"Yes, it is. Now we have to find a substance that can

bring the temperature on Ahi down low enough to destroy those cells."

"Does anything like that exist, Dr. Fleming?" Evans asked.

"There is something," Fleming said slowly, "an experimental cryogenic the army's been working on. It's considered top secret."

"Can we get access to it?" Deborah asked.

"I hope so," he said. "I'm afraid the time has come to bring the White House into this. I'll leave for the mainland tomorrow."

-Eleven-

It had been two days since Dr. Fleming had left for Oahu and Washington. When Ryan and Jenson returned to the house, Keoni was standing in the doorway holding a large basket and his fishing nets.

"Hey, Tom," he grinned. "Did you forget we're going fishing off the black beach today?"

He had forgotten. In all the crises of the Ahi plants it had completely slipped his mind. "Gee, Keoni, I don't think we can do it today," he said. "We're expecting some important bulletins. I've got to stay by the radio."

"Go on," Ryan insisted. "Go out with the kid. I'll take over the radio."

"Are you sure you can handle it?" Jenson asked, half-seriously.

"Hey, I was building those things before you were born, pal," Ryan boasted. "Just' cause I've got a desk job doesn't mean I've lost it. Now get out of here before I take the kid myself."

As they headed for the jeep, Keoni pulled at Jenson's arm. "Tom," he said eagerly, "why don't you invite your friends from the center? I'll bet they'd like to see the black beach too."

Jenson smiled at the boy. He had a good idea which

"friend from the center" Keoni wanted to bring along. "Sure, pal, why not? You wait in the jeep and I'll get them."

He found the two young scientists sitting near the launch, watching the water.

"You guys don't look too busy," he said. "Do you want to join Keoni and me on a picnic?"

Deborah accepted immediately, but Evans hesitated. He had made it clear that he did not think much of Jenson.

"Oh, Ian, think of it as research. Besides, we can't do anything else until Dr. Fleming gets back from Washington."

Reluctantly, Evans followed her to Jenson's jeep. "Just one thing," Jenson warned as they walked. "Don't bring up what's going on in Ahi. I don't want to alarm Keoni or anyone else on the island yet."

As soon as Keoni saw Deborah, his brown eyes lit up and he insisted that she sit in the front next to Jenson.

As they sped along the road toward the black beach, a subdued Deborah whispered the details of Dr. Fleming's trip to Washington while Keoni described the various fauna to Evans.

"You know what I like the most?" Deborah said as they drove through the lush groves.

"What's that?" Tom asked.

"The beautiful names they have given these islands. Do they have any significance?" Deborah asked reflectively.

"Oh, definitely." Tom laughed. "The names usually reflect what the island represents to the people. Ahi, for instant, means island of fire, and Nalowale means lost island. I guess all things considered that pretty well nails it. Look out there," Tom gestured toward a grove of tall stately trees with large purple fruit that looked like stuffed olives.

"Oh, sandalwood," she said, inhaling the delicate fragrance of the wood.

"All these islands used to be covered with them," Jenson said. "But in the late 1700s the monarchy started selling the wood to China and Polynesia. Soon they were trading in it all over the world. By 1925 the forests were completely logged out."

"But they're coming back," she said hopefully, looking back at the grove.

"Yeah," he said dryly. "I just hope Dr. Fleming is right about them not having emotions. If they ever develop a sense of revenge we're in real trouble."

As they gazed out at the black lava road she saw that it was lined with tall spicy smelling reeds of ginger and wild sugar cane. The palm trees were thicker than ever and their coconuts were the size of watermelons.

"The most tragic thing about these plants is that if we could only communicate or control them in some way it would go a long way in solving the food shortages in the world," she said sadly.

They had reached the black beach and Jenson parked the jeep in the shade of the gaudy new rainbow shower trees. The huge fluffy blossoms varied from pale yellow to bold orange making the tree look like a sunburst.

"Hey, Dr. Evans," Keoni announced. "How about if you come down the beach with me and see if we can catch some fish for lunch?"

"That's a good idea, Ian," Deborah agreed. "Tom and

I can set up the hibachi."

Reluctantly, Evans took some of Keoni's nets and followed him down the beach. Deborah watched them go and then turned to Jenson.

He was already putting charcoal in the small stove. He lit it and stepped back as the flames took hold.

"It'll take awhile for it to heat up, but by that time Keoni and Evans should have some fish for us," he said. "Would you like some pineapple while we wait?"

"Sure, did you bring any?"

He laughed. "Look around you, Deborah, I'm sure you can come up with something."

Embarrassed, she looked around. Then she spotted them. The spiky brown fruits were almost hidden by low clusters of leaves. "These pineapples are a foot long," she said breaking one off. It took two hands to carry it.

"I wonder if it's ripe," she said as she brought it back.

"I'll see," Tom volunteered taking it from her. He tapped it with his finger and heard a dull thumping sound against the skin. "A hollow sound means it's not ready, but this baby's full of juice."

He took his knife and began to cut up the fruit. He handed her a piece and she quickly put it in her mouth. It tasted as sweet as sugar. A bright green-and-red macaw watched them with interest from a nearby tibouching bush and Jenson tossed him a piece. The bird deftly caught it in its big yellow beak.

"You know, Tom, I admired the way you handled that incident at Lani's home the other night," she said. "I never had a chance to tell you."

He shrugged. "They're like my own. What happens to them is important to me."

"Then maybe you'll understand how I feel about Dr. Fleming. He's like my own father. It's an honor to be part of his work."

"An honor to be part of this mess?" he said curtly.

She turned on him with anger in her eyes. "You seem to think this is all our fault, Tom. You act as though Dr. Fleming were personally responsible for the deaths and Ian and I were his accomplices."

"Are you?"

"That volcano was an act of nature," she shouted. "It's very nice for you to sunbathe here on your tropical island and pretend that nature is all orchids and palm trees, but it isn't. Nature is volcanoes and floods and tidal waves. It can be ugly and dangerous. We're seeing that side of it now."

"Hey, you don't have to tell me about nature, lady," he shouted back. "But nature didn't turn that island into a breeding ground for alien life forms or seed the crater with radioactive isotopes."

"You're right," she admitted. "But the point is that it was done. Now we have to do our best to deal with the consequences."

"According to your mentor, Dr. Fleming, we may not have the time," he said dryly. Suddenly he grabbed her by the shoulders and stared at her. "I have to know something, Deborah."

"What's that?" She moved her foot idly in the warm water.

"Did you know about all this?"

"About what?"

"About this bizarre testing on Ahi?"

"No," she shook her head. "I had no idea."

"How about the Kaolani Center?" he persisted. "Didn't you know it was a front?"

"No," she said. "I guess I suspected something, but I just convinced myself that Dr. Fleming had a good relationship with the Defense Department. Anytime we needed a plane, a ship, or any equipment, we got it."

"And you never thought about it?"

"Really, Tom," she said, getting back on her feet, "I don't see why I should be on the defensive. What about you? You've been hiding away in your own paradise, sending in your reports, while people like Dr. Fleming were really trying to do something to help mankind. You have no idea of the work that Dr. Fleming and the center have been doing."

"I'm beginning to get some idea."

"Mistakes were made but they were based on the best information available at that time. And he's trying to rectify them," she insisted.

Their argument was cut short by the sight of Keoni running down the beach. "Tom, Tom, come quick," the boy screamed. "Dr. Evans is in trouble."

Jenson put down the charcoal he was about to lay on the hibachi and went running after the boy. Deborah followed. As they caught up with Keoni he breathlessly explained what had happened.

"We had our nets on the shore and we rolled up our pants and waded out into the surf. We were going to get the fish confused and make them head for our nets," he said, pausing a minute to catch his breath. "I went after a grouper; when I turned around, Dr. Evans was down in the water with seaweed all around him. I thought he had fallen, and I started to laugh, but he wasn't laughing.

Man, he was scared."

"Where is he now?" Deborah asked

"He's still down there." The boy pointed toward the sea and suddenly she saw Ian struggling with what looked like a giant clump of seaweed.

"Oh, my God," she screamed as Jenson waded in. When Evans saw him he tried to say something, but he was too weak from struggling to breathe.

"Get out of here," he managed to gasp. "It's going to kill you too."

"We're not leaving you," Jenson yelled as he began to cut away the cold wet tentacles of seaweed with his knife. He struggled to release Evans, and when he was free, he carried him up to the shore.

Evans fought to regain his breath. "Thanks," he said almost reluctantly. "You saved my life."

"Can you walk?" Jenson asked.

"Yeah, I think I'm all right now."

Jenson gave him a hand to get up, but he insisted on walking back to the fire under his own power. Deborah picked up some samples of the strange seaweed and Keoni followed with the three groupers he had managed to trap. That would be enough fish for them.

But when they returned to Jenson's fire another surprise was awaiting them. The air had turned thin and everywhere they could taste the sour flavor of carbon dioxide. The fire was cold.

"I don't understand," Deborah said impatiently. "It was burning fine a few minutes ago."

"Don't you?" Evans said. "It's the plants. They put this fire out the way their friends did on Ahi. Come on, let's get out of here, this place gives me the creeps."

-Twelve-

The Richard Fleming who arrived at the White House looked quite different from the man who had been working at Kaolani Center. His aloha shirt and sandals had been replaced by a banker's dark pinstriped suit and shining black shoes. He carried a custom-made leather briefcase that was locked and chained to his wrist.

He was not looking forward to this meeting. He had failed twice in controlling the Ahi plants and every moment that passed increased the danger. Yet Ahi and Nalowale seemed so far away now and he wondered if he could succeed in convincing the president, safely ensconced in the Oval Office of the White House, that the welfare of the entire world was threatened by an island of plants half a world away.

A young aide met him at the airport and escorted him to the door of the Oval Office. Inside, the president and the secretary of defense were waiting for him. The president was seated at the massive mahogany desk that had once belonged to Andrew Jackson. Behind was the balcony that overlooked the south lawn. Beyond the Oval Office were the private quarters of the President and his family.

Fleming found himself wondering if they had an

influence on his decisions. Certainly today, when he might come very close to affecting the future of the world, he must think about the effect on them.

On the walls of the Oval Office hung several portraits of previous presidents. The desk was bare expect for a silver-framed photograph of a pretty light-haired women and two laughing little girls.

The secretary was seated in one of the brown leather armchairs that faced the desk and he indicated that Fleming should take the other. After some preliminaries, the president spoke.

"I understand that the situation on Ahi is still critical," the president said gravely as Fleming sat down.

"Yes, Mr. President," he acknowledged. "All attempts to control the Ahi entities have failed. Our conventional forms of defense have been totally ineffective. What we must accept is that these plants, as we have been calling them, evolved from the lunar seedpods placed on the island some thirty years ago. Based on what we have observed over the past few days it is entirely possible that these are in fact a sentient life form. If that is the case we must carefully choose our next course of action."

The defense secretary moved restlessly in his chair. He had headed one of the nations, largest computer corporations before accepting the cabinet post. He felt strongly about the military's proprietary issues on defense, and did not believe that "civilians" were qualified to make decisions concerning them.

Fleming continued. "We apparently are dealing with a totally new life form, sir, one whose development may have occurred millions of years ago. Over the years some noted scientists have strongly suggested the connection between what we consider living and "non-living" species, such as humans and plant life, has not fully been explored, and that some form of consciousness may exist in all matter. Other experiments seem to indicate that plants possess a form of awareness or sensitivity to electromagnetic frequencies and waves besides those of visible light provided by the sun. It is difficult to confront potential enemies when we know little about them. So far they have neutralized every attempt we have made to control them. We are like David, armed only with a slingshot."

"Have we had any success in our attempts to communicate with them?" the president asked thoughtfully.

"No, sir. We have been analyzing the sounds and emissions coming from the island, but all attempts to date to link up have failed. Either they don't understand or they are not interested in communicating. The problem we face, sir, is that even here plants have been evolved through incalculable eons of time, and their progress would indicate an inspiring intelligence. Unfortunately, we may not understand even if we do get an answer."

Unlocking his briefcase, Fleming took out his color slides and photographs of the Ahi plants.

"I thought you were going to take care of all this when you fire-bombed the island," the secretary said. "That's why I let you have the *Defiant*. What happened to that?"

"The fire bombing failed, because we simply underestimated the intelligence of these life forms. We assumed that although they were alien to earth, they were just common garden-variety plants. As I said, it is very apparent now that although they strongly resemble our botanical life they are far more than that," Fleming answered with obvious frustration.

"Doctor, I would of course like to communicate with whatever this is if is at all possible. But if it's not I want to be sure we have a way to remove this threat," the president said as he again looked at the slides with interest. Turning back to Fleming he asked, "What do we know so far?"

"Well, sir, after extensive testing my assistant, Dr. Saunders, and I believe we may have found a weak spot. The Ahi plants are extremely sensitive to cold."

The president and the secretary sat up and exchanged glances. They knew what was coming.

"I suggest," Fleming, continued calmly, "that we consider using the XCFG."

"Out of the question," the secretary roared.

"Wait a minute, Jim," the president said raising his hand. "Let him continue."

Fleming paused. He did not blame the secretary for reacting that way. He had expected it. He, too, had resisted using XCFG at first. Army scientists working on super-conductive materials and cryogenics had isolated the new freezing agent, but so far it had only been used in laboratories and its total effectiveness was unknown.

"So far the only thing that seems to significantly weaken the Ahi plants is cold," Fleming explained. "When the plants are exposed to cold, ice crystals form in the spaces between the cells, withdrawing water from the cells and drying and deforming them. As far as we know, none of the Ahi plants has any resistance to the formation of ice crystals. They may all be vulnerable."

"Do you suggest we freeze the entire island?" the president asked.

"I fully realize the gravity of my request," Fleming assured the two men.

"Do you, Doctor?" the secretary asked cautiously. "Do you know what premature exposure of XCFG could mean to the United States?"

Fleming knew the meeting would not be easy but he had promised himself he would not yield to anger. But, in spite of his promise, he could feel the frustration building within him.

"If something isn't done to stop the life form now existing on Ahi, Mr. Secretary," he said firmly, "there may be no United States or any other place to worry about."

The president stared at the colored slides again. "What a shame," he mused. "The plants are remarkably beautiful. God only knows how old they are and what they are capable of doing."

"Yes, Mr. President. The Island of Ahi is now one of the most beautiful places I have ever seen in my life. But whatever they are we know that at least five people have already been killed. They apparently care not for boundaries, nations, race, or ideology. All they know is that they must survive."

"How much XCFG would you need to saturate Ahi?" The President's tone was almost casual.

"I estimate a hundred kiloliters would do."

The president turned to the secretary. "How long would that take you to produce, Jim?"

"Two weeks."

"We don't have two weeks, Jim," he said briskly. "I want a hundred kiloliters of XCFG on its way to Ahi seven days from today."

"Yes, Mr. President."

The president turned back to Fleming. "Is there anything else?"

Fleming nodded. "We cannot be sure that these unusual developments are limited to the island. There's been a build-up of seaweed off the coast of Nalowale and it may be connected to the Ahi plants. I request permission to use the *Seeker* to reconnoiter deep-sea activities in the Ahi area. The *Seeker* will also provide us with detailed mapping and surveillance through its access to the ORION Satellite System."

"What do you say to that, Jim?" the president asked the secretary.

The secretary's face showed his concern

"We can provide the *Seeker*," he acknowledged.

"Good." The president smiled. "James Boyes is captain of the Seeker. He's a good man and the *Seeker* is the newest and best-equipped submersible in the fleet. I hope it can put an end to this, fast."

Fleming sighed with relief. They were on their way.

-Thirteen-

Two days later Dr. Fleming arrived on the USS *Seeker*. The nuclear submarine anchored two miles off the shore of Nalowale and he returned to the island with the captain and the executive officer, Captain James Boyes and Commander Jack Lee. Both men wore the twin silver dolphins of trained submariners. Together they made their way to Jenson's house, and there Deborah, Evans, and Fleming briefed them on the importance of the planned operation while Mike Ryan and Jenson listened.

"First," Fleming told them, "we will reconnoiter the deep-sea area around Ahi, then we will move in with the cryogenic."

"How soon can you be ready to sail, Captain Boyes?" Deborah asked.

"The *Seeker* can sail any time, Dr. Saunders," he assured her. "She's always ready for immediate action."

"Now let me get this straight, Dr. Fleming," Mike Ryan said. "I'm to remain here and once you're submerged you'll set up communications with me from aboard the *Seeker*?"

"That's right, Mike," Fleming said. "The *Seeker* is equipped with a new low frequency radio system that permits us to communicate from several hundred feet below the surface."

Satisfied that the briefing was complete, Captain Boyes and Commander Lee rose to leave.

"Just one more thing, gentlemen," Fleming continued. "When you brief your crew about this mission, please remember that above all we want to avoid any panic."

"That's understood, Dr. Fleming," Boyes assured him. "We'll see you all in the morning."

The following morning at dawn four tense civilians boarded the awaiting *Seeker* and Commander Lee offered to show them around the submarine before they descended.

The boat resembled a conventional submarine in appearance. It was four hundred feet long with eight forward torpedo tubes. On top was the conning tower, which housed the retracting periscopes, radar, radio antennas, and snorkel tubes.

"Today we use the conning tower as the bridge," Commander Lee noted. "We rely more on the sonar than the periscope."

The commander led them through the tightly fitted boat. Every inch of space was used to its best advantage, beginning with the stern where the nuclear plant was housed. This consisted of an atomic reactor that generated enormous heat through nuclear fission. Inserting and withdrawing control rods that penetrated the reactor core, Lee explained, controlled the reactor.

"The advantages of nuclear power are enormous," Lee said. "This sub is capable of remaining underwater for six months at a time, and we don't need to surface for oxygen to operate.

"All nuclear subs have auxiliary diesel electrical machinery," he added, "in case of failure or when we shut down the reactor in port."

As they moved through the narrow corridor, Deborah noticed that chrome loops hung from the ceiling at regular intervals, she asked about them.

"Oh, you'll understand once we're underway." He smiled. "You'll be looking around for something to grab onto and there they'll be."

They passed through a small laboratory and computer room, the crews quarters, and a galley where the cook was already preparing spaghetti for lunch.

"How many men do you have on board, commander?" Deborah asked.

"We have a hundred men, mostly petty officers," Lee said. "You need a pretty sophisticated sailor on a boat like this." He paused at a door with a sign that said "Munitions Room."

"Inside here are the self-propelled torpedoes," he said. "They're specially designed for this boat. We have subrocs, which can be fired from the torpedo tubes, they shoot into the air, arc at about thirty miles per hour toward their targets, and detonate a nuclear warhead. That's another advantage of the nuclear sub. We can fire nuclear missiles without surfacing, which makes it the most important of our strategic weapons. We also have top antiship and antisub missiles."

The next door had a big red sign on it that said "Off Limits, Authorized Personnel Only." Immediately Deborah and Jenson asked about it.

"I can only tell you that inside is a weapon that we

hope will make nuclear weapons obsolete," Lee said, and moved them along quickly through the officers' mess and quarters to the bow.

The bow of the *Seeker* was made up of the control room and a small forward observation compartment. The control room housed sonar detection equipment, a complex inertial navigational system, and port and starboard cameras that projected images onto a television screen.

"The sonar emits a continuous pulse," Lee said as he gestured toward the sonar screen which was sounding a steady beep. "Years ago we had to record that on tape and analyze it on land. Now we can analyze it on board immediately."

"I bet there are a lot of sounds to measure down here," Jenson said.

"Oh, yes," the commander assured him. "In fact it was submarine sonar that first made us aware of the world of underwater sound. The sea is every bit as noisy as land."

"Oh, really?" Jenson smiled. "How come I never hear it?"

"Because the air-water interface acts as a sound barrier so that noises from one world hardly penetrate the other. Actually, whales and porpoises are very talkative, as are many fish. Even invertebrates make unique noises and we suspect that they're not just communication. They may be using sound to navigate the way we use sonar." The young commander went on to describe how sound actually traveled five times faster through water than air.

The control board itself was a maze of red and green lights and to Jenson the whole thing looked not unlike a floor-to-ceiling version of an airplane cockpit.

Completing the image were two young officers strapped into bucket seats.

"Actual control of the *Seeker* is in the hands of these two," Lee said. "They drive the boat."

"Drive?" Deborah asked.

"That's right, you don't sail a submarine, you drive it, and it's a boat not a ship." Lee smiled. Suddenly a red warning light began to flash. "Every one of these lights represents a specific opening or superstructure," he explained, pointing at the panel. "Green means closed and water tight, red indicates still open. Everything will be green when we descend." He gestured at the rest of the board. "These wheels control our diving planes and the levers will control flooding and emptying the ballast tanks."

The captain gave the order to begin the descent.

As the *Seeker* began its descent the lights switched from red to green until the whole panel was green.

The water ballast tanks were flooded to attain neutral buoyancy. Next the diving planes on either side of the boat began a rotating motion as the *Seeker* dived forward. The impact jolted Deborah and she almost fell before she remembered the hooks. She clung to one tightly as the boat gradually regained its trim.

"Keep an eye out for any change in the mass around Ahi," Captain Boyes cautioned the pilot. "The lava flow from that volcano has probably caused a lot of changes on the ocean floor."

"Aye, aye, sir," the pilot said. "The scanners indicate the new lava flow beneath Ahi has extended 150 meters. That last eruption must have caused a major breach in the southeast flank of the summit. There's a hole about fifty meters around."

"Good work," Boyes said. "I don't want to get sandwiched in there."

"Sir," the diving officer addressed the captain, "we're at fifty feet and can begin further descent at any time. The radio room is maintaining an open channel to Ryan on Nalowale."

Boyes turned to Dr. Fleming. "Well, doctor, we'll hold at fifty feet awhile and begin further descent whenever you're ready."

"Thank you, captain. Let's hold at this depth for a while as we circle the island."

"Commander," Boyes addressed Lee, "turn on the forward cameras and open the protective bow doors so we can get a look out there.

"Aye, aye, sir."

Fleming, Deborah, Evans, and Boyes proceeded to the forward observation compartment. In front of them two huge view ports allowed a spectacular view of the ocean depths. A boom extended from the bow of the *Seeker*. It was lined with high intensity tungsten iodide lights to illuminate the depths.

"It's simply unbelievable," Deborah said as she gazed out. "It's like looking into another world, it's so beautiful and peaceful." The lights of the *Seeker* hit varicolored fish that glowed like blue-white stars in the darkness of the deep ocean. Some were moving on their own power and others seemed to drift with the current.

"That's exactly what it is," said Dr. Fleming, "a world we seldom see. And it's 70 percent of the earth, so it's a significant world indeed."

For an hour and a half the *Seeker* moved slowly through the waters around Ahi. Except for some heavy sea growth there did not appear to be any significant changes. Fleming suggested that they investigate further and Boyes gave the order to dive 150 feet.

Hold at one-five-zero," yelled the diving officer.

"One-five-zero and holding, sir."

"Engine room, all ahead one-third."

"All ahead one-third. Aye, aye, captain."

"Can you have the cameras swing around to the starboard?" Dr. Fleming asked. "I want to have a closer look at that mass out there."

"Can do, doctor," Boyes said. He turned to the intercom. "Activate starboard cameras, optimum magnification."

Floating by the view port was a strange mass of brown seaweed that seemed to be several hundred feet wide.

"Will you look at that?" Deborah said. "What do make of it, Dr. Fleming?"

"I don't know. It may be a new species of kelp," he said slowly."

"Captain Boyes, do you have any external scoops aboard? I'd like to snare some of that thing and give it a closer look."

"Yes, Dr. Fleming, the *Seeker* is equipped with two ten-foot long hydraulically operated mechanical arms that can lift sample plants and stow them in a metal basket below the bow. Each arm can lift five thousand pounds, but has the dexterity to pick up a pencil." Boyes turned to Commander Lee. "See to it that the scoops get some samples from that mass of kelp out there."

"Aye, aye, sir," Lee replied. He left the observation deck for the *Seeker*'s laboratory. In the corridor he bumped into Jenson.

"How's it going up there?" he asked with a broad smile. "See any mermaids?"

"No mermaids, but there are funny-looking things out there that Dr. Fleming wants to take a closer look at."

"Watch it, commander," Jenson cautioned. "I took a chunk out of one of those fast-growing beasties on land and it damned near took my hand off."

Commander Lee smiled. "I'll keep that in mind."

Jenson found Fleming and Deborah in the observation deck gazing out the view port.

"Damn!" he exclaimed. "What a magnificent view!"

"I hope we'll have an opportunity to reach the ocean floor," Dr. Fleming told him. "There you'll see magnificent huge sea anemones that can eat a shark, and sloping sandy planes sprinkled with red coral."

"You sound like a travel brochure," Deborah teased.

The older man shrugged. "I suppose it is my favorite place, Deborah. Its beauty is unmatched by anything I've ever seen in the world."

The odd brownish-green mass of kelp floated by the view port again.

"Is that the thing Commander Lee was just telling me about?" Jenson asked.

"That's it," Evans said grimly. "Don't some of the leaves look familiar?"

The three others stared out at the kelp. Its huge tentacles included the odd heart-shaped leaves they had first seen on the Ahi plants.

"That's impossible," Deborah shook her head. "They

may look similar, but kelp is an algae, it can't have anything like the leaf structure of a land plant."

Fleming put his arm on her shoulder in a supportive gesture. "I'm afraid, Deborah, that with these strange life forms anything is possible. We must have an open mind." He looked back at the strange mass. "Whatever it is, it's definitely a living entity and probably one of a very high order."

Suddenly the intercom crackled with a message. "Sonar to observation deck."

"Captain Boyes here."

"Sir, we're picking up an echo. It appears to be a large mass of some sort."

"Where is it?"

"Below us. Bearing zero-one-zero; range a thousand yards. It appears to be stationary."

"What do you make of it?"

"I don't know, sir. It doesn't read like anything I've ever bounced sonar off of before, but whatever it is, it's a pretty good size."

"Keep an eye on it, sonar, and give me a 360 degree sweep."

"Aye, aye, sir."

"Science lab to captain," the voice of Commander Lee came across the intercom.

"Go ahead, commander."

"Sir, we're ready to pick up the samples."

Boyes switched to the engine room, ordered the ship stopped, and switched back to Lee. "Okay, anytime you're ready."

He turned back to the three scientists and Jenson. "If you look over there at the nose camera you should be able to see the scoops at work."

Fleming moved toward the intercom and addressed Lee. "Have those scoops move in as gently as possible, commander. We're not sure what the reaction of whatever that is out there may be."

The others watched with awe as the huge projectors delicately poked at the mass of kelp.

"There," Fleming said. "They've made contact. They've cut away a piece of the kelp."

"Radio room to captain." The intercom came alive again.

"Go ahead, sparks."

"Sir, we're picking up heavy interference on the radio."

"Dr. Fleming," Evans shouted. "Look at that kelp." The brownish-green seaweed had begun to vibrate and unravel, obscuring everything else from the view port. "It's spreading like crazy!"

"Tom, you'd better get down to the radio room and see if we're still in contact with Ryan."

"I'm on my way, doctor."

But as he turned to leave the observation deck the *Seeker* was suddenly tossed about as if it had been hit broadside. Power and communications stopped, plunging the boat into total silence and darkness for ten seconds.

When the lights came on again, Boyes called the bridge. "What happened?" he asked.

"According to the computer, sir," the bridge officer reported, "we were hit with a very sophisticated form of subsonic wave."

"Subsonic?"

"That's right, sir. Well into the subsonic range."

"Any idea where it came from?"

"Yes, sir. It came from whatever that thing is out there."

"That ball of seaweed?" the captain asked.

"I know it sounds far-out, captain," the officer acknowledged, "but that's what the computer prints. The radio room says that just prior to the hit there was extreme distortion on the radio. Sparks said the squeal almost knocked his earphones off."

"Okay," Boyes sighed. "Keep me posted."

"Aye, aye, sir."

Boyes turned to Dr. Fleming. "You heard what he said, Dr. Fleming. Is that possible?"

"I'm afraid it's all too possible." The older man shook his head.

"You know, when the secretary of defense told Commander Lee and me that this was going to be a different type of research mission, I didn't envision anything like this."

"I dare say, captain, that this will probably be the most unusual research mission you'll ever see. How we handle ourselves in the next few minutes may determine if we come back from it."

"Look, Doctor, what is it we're up against?" he asked. "Lee and I had a lot of briefing from Washington, but quite frankly we weren't prepared for anything like this. The secretary kept talking about this plant life and the escalation that's taking place on Ahi and he told us we were out here to look for something new and different, but just what it was he didn't say."

"Well, I think you've found it," Jenson said as he

continued to stare out at the object that had nearly destroyed them all. "I'm going down to the communication center now, Dr. Fleming and see if I can get Ryan on the horn."

"Good idea, Tom," Fleming agreed. "We'd better let him know what's happening here." As Jenson left, he turned to the captain. "Were we able to get those plant samples aboard?"

"Yes, Dr. Fleming, they've got them in the isolation tank now."

"I want to take a look at them as soon as possible."

"Okay, doctor. Follow me." He paused at the intercom. "Bridge, this is the captain."

"Bridge, aye, sir."

"Secure the safety doors on the observation deck, maintain full sonar surveillance, and let's go to general quarters. I don't know how that thing out there did what it did to us, but if it decides to move again I want to be ready for it. If you need me, I'll be in the lab with Dr. Fleming."

"Right, captain."

The intercom was already buzzing when they arrived in the lab. It was the sonar operator.

"Sir, that stationary object we've been observing is beginning to move. Right toward us."

"What's its range now?" Boyes asked.

"About five hundred yards, sir, still bearing zero-one-zero."

"Continue to keep a close eye on it," he ordered. "Let me know every move it makes."

"Aye, aye, sir."

Boyes switched to the bridge. "This is the captain,"

he said. "Activate the bow cameras and give me a full swing. Then zero in on that object." He turned back to Dr. Fleming. "Maybe you should have a look at this, too. I don't know what's going on out there, but I've got a funny feeling that this is going to be just as strange as that last thing."

"You may be right, captain."

They returned to the bridge as the bow cameras picked up the approaching object.

"Sonar," Boyes shouted over the intercom, "what do you make of this?"

"It's like nothing I've ever seen before, captain," the voice answered. "It's immense. I would say it's a couple of hundred feet across and maybe fifty feet high."

"Sir," Commander Lee called from the view port, "that object is getting closer."

"Okay, give me full magnification on the cameras."

"Coming up, sir."

"Oh my God!" Deborah screamed. "What's that?"

All eyes on the observation deck suddenly focused on the image on the screen. Long stringing tentacles went out one hundred and two hundred feet from a broad core at the center that resembled a thick stalk of celery. It was gliding through the water toward the *Seeker*.

"Helmsman!" Boyes ordered. "Right full rudder. Ahead one-third."

"Rudder is full right, sir."

"Brace yourselves," Boyes told the scientists. "It's going to be a little rough out there." He turned back to the intercom. "Come to new course, one-nine-zero." Next he addressed the sonar operator. "What is that thing's bearing?"

"Sir, it seems to be moving with us. As we turn it turns and now it's blocking our path."

"That's impossible."

"Maybe so, sir, but it's happening."

"Come around to new course, two-eight-zero."

"Sir, we are picking up another object, aft."

"Same type?"

"Yes, sir. It appears to be the same type, but smaller."

"Looks like we might have a bit of a problem," he said dryly.

"Sir."

"Yes, sonar. Two more objects, one to starboard and one to port.

"It looks like we're surrounded," Captain Boyes said. "What's our depth?"

"One hundred and fifty feet, sir."

"Commander!" Boyes called for Lee. "Come to the bridge. I'm going to find an opening and get us the hell out of here."

"Aye, aye, sir."

"Helmsman, right full rudder. Come to new course zero-five-zero, all ahead, full."

"Aye, aye, sir. Zero-five-Zero, all ahead full."

"Sir, the two objects to port and starboard are both converging with us on an intercept course."

"Secure all crash doors!" Boyes ordered. "Stand by for collisions!"

"Sir!" Commander Lee's voice came back on the intercom. "Contact in ten seconds . . . five, four, hold on! We're going to hit!"

As the boat and the huge writhing kelp collided the boat shook violently, throwing Fleming across the floor.

"All stop! All stop!" Boyes ordered.

"Aye, aye, sir. All engines stop."

"Engine room, what is your status?"

"We have power, sir," the answer came. "The reactor is holding steady."

A dazed Dr. Fleming tried to pick himself up from the deck. His right temple was cut and bleeding.

"Dr. Fleming, are you all right?" Deborah asked as she knelt beside him and began to dab at the wound.

"I don't know," he said weakly.

"You should lie down."

"No." He was emphatic. "I must stay here."

Suddenly on the screen in front of them they could see the huge tentacles holding the *Seeker* in their grip. The huge submarine seemed like a child's toy.

"Sir," the voice of Commander Lee came across the intercom. "Damage control reports slight damage in the aft compartments. Observation deck is intact; safety doors caught the brunt of the impact. Most of the damage to the aft seems to have been caused by secondary impact in that area."

Boyes switched to the communications center.

"Are you able to make contact with Nalowale?"

"No sir, we're completely out of business down here. We're being jammed on all frequencies."

Jenson turned back to the undulating mass on the screen. "What's that damned thing doing out there?"

"It's pulling us down, sir. Whatever it is it's taking us down."

The boat rapidly dropped, reaching three hundred feet.

Fleming joined him at the screen. "I don't know

what's

happening, but whatever it is, it's not good."

The voice of the sonar operator was back. "Sir," he said anxiously, "sonar is malfunctioning. I'm getting objects and echoes all over the place, I can't be sure what's real and what isn't. Whatever is out there, it's not only holding us, it's jamming our communications and slowly pulling us to the bottom."

Deborah moved back into the observation compartment and stared out the view ports. They had reached the ocean floor. The

greenish silt bottom was shifting like the sands of a windy desert. Long thin rattail fish a foot long moved about the dark water as elegant starfish clung to the branches of stalky golden sea pens.

"Look at those lobsters," Evans shouted as a parade of five passed by. "They must be three feet long."

A varicolored mass of plankton shining red, yellow, green, and blue in the tungsten light of the *Seeker* floated by. Then

suddenly the view changed. A dead jellyfish floated by and then Deborah counted ten dead squid on the ocean floor. The white corpses were each surrounded by an ugly black border.

"That's a bad sign." She shook her head.

"Why?" Jenson asked.

"Fish need oxygen as much as we do, Tom," she said. "And that black border suggests that there's no oxygen in this atmosphere. Notice how totally still it is?"

"Yes."

"I'm afraid the plants down here are manufacturing carbon dioxide too, just as we feared," she said and then turned toward the control room. “I'd better tell Dr. Fleming.”

Inside the control room Captain Boyes had come to a decision. Turning to Fleming he said, “torpedoes are out of the question at this range. Our only chance may be the HPM generator. You realize, doctor, we won’t have to get authorization to use it, but if we don’t we’re all history.

“I understand and appreciate your taking the step,” Fleming assured him gravely.

Boyes picked up the intercom. “Engine room, can you still deliver power?” he demanded.

“Yes, sir. The reactor is holding. No drop in power.”

“Fine. When I call for it give me everything you've got, all back emergency.”

“Aye, aye, sir. On your signal.”

Boyes switched to the laboratory. “This is the captain. Is the HPM generator on line?”

“Yes, sir.”

“Good. Open deflector doors and bring us to half-energy level. Prepare to fire.”

“Aye, aye, sir.”

“What's the HPM generator, captain?” Jenson asked.

“It is our newest weapon, an advanced highly sophisticated High Power Microwave generator. The pulse produces a powerful electromagnetic field. When fired it will send a brief charge of several thousand volts through the isolated outer hull of the boat. Hopefully, whatever that thing is out there it will be thrown clear or at least weakened enough for us to pull free.”

“Like a laser?” Deborah asked.

“Much more then that,” Boyes replied. “It has far more penetrating power but without the heat dissipation that the laser would transmit."

Fleming nodded. "That should do it."

"I hope so, doctor. Whatever that is, it's holding us down. We could survive for a while under normal circumstances but if that thing begins to exert pressure against the hull it could crush us even before we reach burst depth." He turned back to the intercom. "Engine room ready?"

"Aye, sir. Engine room ready."

"Lab?"

"Lab, aye, aye, sir."

"Is the HPM charged to half yet?"

"Yes, sir."

"Deflection doors open, pulse at half charge," he ordered. "Attention engine room, stand by, we're going to hit that thing with the HPM."

"Aye, aye, sir."

"Stand by lab."

"Aye, sir. Laboratory standing by."

The three scientists and Jenson stared at each other. They realized that their fate now rested with Captain Boyes. His control and understanding of the *Seeker* were their only weapons against the plant.

"Attention all hands," Boyes addressed the entire crew of the *Seeker*. "This is the captain speaking. We are now 370 feet down and some form of plant life, which we cannot identify, is dragging us. Whatever it is, it's extremely powerful and we are presently entangled in its tentacles. In thirty seconds we're going to charge the outer hull. I don't know what its reaction will be so I want everybody on their toes. We'll maintain 'general quarters' until this present threat has been overcome." He paused to let the message sink in. “Science lab, commence firing.”

“Aye, aye sir.”

Deborah, Jenson, and Dr. Fleming hovered over the screen as the powerful charge struck the awesome creature. It reeled violently, its tentacle arms flailing through the water. Then close to the top of the stalk center there appeared a large split like an open wound from which oozed a thick, black sap.

For a few brief moments the grip of the plant seemed to ease; then it recovered itself and its huge tentacles again began crushing the hull of the *Seeker* and dragging it across the ocean bottom.

“Engine room,” Boyes shouted into the intercom. “Do we still have reactor power?”

“Yes, sir,” they assured him. “But the hull pressure is increasing.”

“I know. Our angle of descent was very steep. Maintain trim and stabilize the reactor. Be ready to give me everything we've got when I ask for it.”

As they watched the mass thrashing silently in the water, Deborah sought Jenson's hand. They looked up to see

Commander Lee standing in the doorway holding a sheaf of printouts.

“I've got a read-out on the damage, captain,” he announced. “The beam apparently weakened that thing considerably, but not enough to shake it loose.”

“That's what I was afraid of,” Boyes said and turned to Dr. Fleming. “How much power do you estimate it would take to neutralize that thing?”

Fleming shook his head. “I can only give you an

opinion. I'd say if we take another shot we should hit it with everything we've got."

"Looks like we're going to have to close the book again if we ever want to surface, Jack," Boyes said. "I want you to go down to engineering and when I call for it back us out of here with every ounce of power you can muster."

"Aye, aye, sir," Lee said. "The power will be there when you need it."

"Thanks, Lee, and good luck." He picked up the intercom again and addressed the entire ship. "Attention, this is the captain speaking. In one minute we're going to discharge the HPM again, this time at full power. At the same time we're going to pull away and back out of the grasp of that thing. It may turn out to be pretty rough, so hang on to something and brace yourselves."

Next he spoke directly to the laboratory. "Stand by to fire at full power."

"Aye, aye, sir."

"Commence firing."

As the beam was fired the submarine was tossed with a tremendous jolt. And then the object reeled and shook violently as it began to come apart.

"Engine room, all back emergency," Boyes shouted.

"Engine room, aye," came the reply. "All back emergency."

For the next thirty seconds the plant and the *Seeker* were locked in a life-and-death struggle. The creature had been dealt a crippling blow, but even in its weakened state it continued to hold onto its prey as the *Seeker* struggled to break from its grip. After what seemed like an eternity the *Seeker* suddenly jerked free and began to move away from its captor. The cameras showed some distance appearing between them and the creature they had just left behind.

"Helm, this is the captain, come around to new course, one-eight-zero, all ahead half."

"Aye, aye, sir. New course one-eight-zero, all ahead half."

"Commander, get me a full damage report and a list of any casualties."

"Aye, aye, sir."

Boyes seemed to relax for the first time in an hour, as he turned to Dr. Fleming. "Well, what do you think of all that?"

"It's even worse than I expected, captain. But it does prove our theory that the source of our problem has been coming from deep within Ahi Island. Now it's affected the sea life. Whatever it is, it appears to be located around here. I don't think that will be the case for long, however. That mutated form we just encountered is a crossbreed of plant life that is probably millions of years advanced from anything now on Earth. It is, in a sense, an almost thinking, reasoning creature. Its instinct is still plant life but its desire for survival is far greater than anything we have ever seen before."

"Why did it attack us, doctor?" Boyes asked.

"Because we provoked it."

"You mean the samples we took?"

"Exactly! We attempted to take a sample of a living thing and it simply defended itself."

"That's still fantastic!" Boyes said. "This is the best-equipped, fastest, and most powerful nuclear submarine in the world, and five minutes ago it came very close to crushing us like a cardboard box."

"Captain, you were fighting it in its own world. No matter how strong we are, we're still at a disadvantage outside our normal environment."

Commander Lee was back, looking more anxious than ever.

"Sir," he addressed Boyes, "take a look at this read-out."

Boyes looked at it and passed it to Fleming. "Our underwater probes are registering a significant change in the thermocline layer, Dr. Fleming," he said. "The cold layer has risen to about three hundred feet below the surface. The normal reading for this area is well below fifteen hundred feet."

Fleming shook his head as he passed the read-out to Deborah. "That would explain that mutation," he sighed. "It's ironic, isn't it? It looks as if nature had presented us with a major new energy source and we're going to have to destroy it."

"Whoa, back up," Jenson said. "What are you talking about? What's a thermocline layer?"

"I'll try to explain quickly and simply, Tom. The thermocline layer is the oceanic water layer in which water temperature decreases rapidly with increasing depth. It usually begins about 660 feet down from the relatively warm surface layer and lasts more than 2,500 feet."

"The deep waters below the thermocline layer decrease in temperature much more gradually toward the sea floor," Deborah added.

"That's right." Fleming nodded. "Under normal circumstances the deeper and colder waters are much richer in nutrients and aquatic life forms. Plant life at the lower depths usually gets more sparse due to the lack of available light."

"You say usually," Jenson noted. "Meaning this is different?"

"Yes. It appears that nature has changed the rules. These genetically advanced plants have the ability to produce a form of thermo-chemical energy. In its earlier stages this new force apparently raised the level of the nutrient-rich colder waters several hundred meters closer to the surface--well within the photic zone where the sun is most abundant."

"This movement provided the plant life with two major elements: light and nutrients," Deborah added. "Couple that with the rapid genetic progression and we've got the mutated plant form that almost destroyed the *Seeker*."

"I guess that leaves us only one alternative, Dr. Fleming," Jensen said slowly.

"Yes," the older man agreed. "The bombardment of XCFG must come off on schedule. We can't afford any delay."

"Do you still think that will be effective after what we just saw?"

"We must turn the tide somewhere. If we can neutralize it on the land we may sufficiently reduce the threat in that area. Then we can concentrate on the undersea plants. We're simply not prepared to fight on two fronts and we would be at an even greater disadvantage if we attempted to take on the sea plants before we destroyed those on the land. We'll move in on Ahi tomorrow."

-Fourteen-

Jenson returned to Nalowale with Dr. Fleming, Evans, and Deborah to prepare for the mission to Ahi. Fortunately, no turbulence or storm activity was expected for at least forty-eight hours. Any sudden squall or turbulence would affect the crucial diffusion of the cryogenic gas.

Twice before, they had failed to make any impact on the Ahi plants. Once again aircraft from the *Defiant* would be used, this time to drop the XCFG on the island, and Fleming and his cohorts would monitor the operation on Jenson's radio in a three-way communications arrangement with the *Defiant* and the *Seeke*r.

At six in the morning Jenson stood on the lanai, now almost covered with bright purple bougainvillea, and watched through the telescope as the flight of helicopters lifted off from the carrier *Defiant* toward Ahi. Suddenly a pilot's voice crackled over the radio.

"This is Iceman One to base. Do you read me?"

"This is base station, Iceman, we read you five by. Contact us when you are on station."

"Roger, base. Iceman One out."

A few minutes later the voice was back on the air.

"Iceman One to base, all positions on station."

"Roger, Iceman One. Release your canisters." In succession each of the ten helicopters in the squadron released its canisters of XCFG. Each detonated as it struck the ground releasing a cloud of freezing gas.

Soon a blue-white cloud of ice and mist hung low and motionless over the island. The winds were calm and the only thing visible above the ice cloud was the black brooding volcano crater.

"Now all we can do is wait," Fleming sighed.

The next hour seemed to creep by; yet no one ventured further than the lanai. No one wanted to break contact with the mission helicopters as they waited for the results of the cryogenic gas. Deborah and Evans scanned the portable sensing devices that had been brought to Tom's house from the launch. These devices were now receiving information from the computers on board the *Seeker*, which was preparing to submerge off the island of Ahi, and was receiving data from the remote sensing devices that were placed by U.D.T. teams at Dr. Fleming's request.

Suddenly Deborah noticed something. "Look at this, Dr. Fleming," she called out. "The frequency sensors indicate a weakening of the transmission signal. The signal that's been influencing the Nalowale plants is fading."

"That's something," Fleming agreed, perking up for the first time in days. "Keep an eye on it."

Another hour passed. The signals weakened steadily.

"There does seem to be a change here," Ryan noted. "I don't know if it's actually a loss of signal or simply a change in frequency."

"Well, Tom," said Deborah, "what do you think?"

"I don't know," he admitted. "This is the damnedest operation I've ever seen."

"Hey, look at this," Evans announced. "Everything's gone quiet on Ahi. Whatever it is, it's gone. We destroyed it!" He was beaming.

"It seems that way," Ryan agreed reluctantly. "But it happened awfully damned quick. Something doesn't quite fit."

"We'd better wait a while, Ian," Fleming cautioned, "before we pronounce the Ahi plants dead."

Evans reluctantly returned to his monitor, as all their eyes zeroed in on the sensing devices, waiting for any change on Ahi and praying there would be none.

"Dr. Fleming," Deborah broke the silence. "the thermal sensors are beginning to react."

He looked concerned. "Heat could be a lot of trouble now," he said gravely. "Check with the observation aircraft, Tom, and see if they have anything."

"Iceman One, come in please," Jenson called.

"This is Iceman One, over Ahi."

"Do you see any change in ice-cloud formation?"

"No change at this time," the pilot reported. "But the density of the ice cloud is preventing us from observing the island surface. Estimated temperature down close to zero."

"Roger, Iceman One. Advise us of any change in that cloud." Jenson signed off.

Deborah was becoming more concerned. According to her monitors the temperature on Ahi was continuing to rise.

"Rise? How?" Evans queried "There's enough cold air over there to freeze hell over twice."

"Nevertheless, Ian, it's rising."

"That may not be impossible, Ian," Fleming cautioned. "Remember Ahi is a volcanic island and anything could trigger it."

"Iceman One calling Nalowale, Iceman One calling Nalowale," the pilot's voice sounded frantic.

Jenson turned back to the radio controls. "Come in, Iceman One."

"The cloud is beginning to dissipate," the disbelieving voice came back.

"Dissipate?" Jenson almost yelled.

"That's right; there's no wind, but the temperature on the island is heating up. The cloud's just melting away."

Everyone in the room turned to Dr. Fleming.

The cryogenic gas had been their last hope. Now it, too, seemed to be failing.

"Dr. Fleming," Deborah said, "the signals are coming in again. They're a different type, but they're quite strong."

"It's the plants," Fleming muttered. "They've altered their signals to produce a heat effect. They're melting the cloud. Somehow, they've reversed the photosynthesis process and they're creating heat energy hot enough to melt the cryogenic cloud."

"I think I know how," Deborah said watching the Co2 recorder. "The dioxide level is above 3000 ppm and the temperature is rising at an incredible rate."

"At this rate that cloud won't last another hour," Evans added. "And when it's gone it will mean we've failed."

The voice of the observation helicopter was back on the line. "Iceman One to Nalowale, Iceman One to

Nalowale. The ice cloud is totally gone. Your plants are still there."

Fleming took the mike. "Iceman One, do you note any other changes?"

"Do I!" the voice came back. "It's like a hothouse down here. I can't get within one hundred feet of the surface because of the heat."

Fleming handed the mike back to Jenson. Now he understood. These incredible strange new entities were bathing their wounds and shielding themselves from the enemy until they recovered from the latest attack. They were bloody, but unbowed.

Jenson continued contact with the helicopter as it moved away from the surface of Ahi and higher up in the air. Soon it was on a level with the volcano crater itself

"Hey, you guys should see this," the voice of Iceman One said. "There something going on in the crater."

"He's right," Evans said". "The seismograph indicates activity in the area of the crater.

"Is the pressure building up, Ian?" Fleming asked nervously.

"No, but something is happening," Evans replied.

"See if you can reach the *Seeker*," Fleming said with urgency in his voice. "They must be below the surface of Ahi by now."

"*Seeker*, come in," Jenson said. "Come in, Seeker."

"*Seeker* here." The voice of Sparks was barely distinguishable amid the interference. "Come in, Nalowale."

"Any activity below surface in your area?" Jenson asked.

"You bet," sparks said. The island is boiling like a pot of goulash and our probes are picking up heavy turbulence. Our sensors have detected large deposits of methane hydrate. It looks like the tectonic action has opened up the deposit and it is now venting large volumes of methane gas up towards the base of the crater."

"Methane hydrate?" Fleming said out loud. "That could be real trouble."

"How so?" Jenson asked apprehensively.

"Methane hydrate in deep sea water is an icy substance that forms when methane gas combines with water molecules. When a fracture occurs an undersea tremor such as we are witnessing can release a massive amount of methane gas."

"So what exactly are we looking at, doctor?"

"The methane gas being lighter than air and being produced in great volume will expand rapidly to possibly 150 times its mass. At which time it will explode."

"One hell of way to go," Ryan said rising from his chair and pouring himself a shot of Irish whiskey.

Jenson turned to Dr. Fleming. "Doctor, if Ahi blows again, it's going to send a tidal surge that will cover most of this island."

The voice of Iceman One was back on the line.

"Nalowale," he called.

"Come in, Iceman One."

"Activity in the crater is increasing, and heat has risen considerably."

"Can you get a closer look inside the crater?" asked Fleming. "I must know what is happening in there."

"No, sir, we can't get any closer, there is too much heat and turbulence around the crater."

"How about the surface, Iceman One?" Evans asked.

"Have any fissures appeared?"

"Not that we can see."

"Understood, Iceman One."

"Doctor," Deborah called out. "I'm still getting signals across the island. But there has been a sharp increase in level from the crater."

"What the hell is going on down there?" Jenson asked, raising his hands in the air in frustration.

"Tom, contact the *Seeker*, tell Captain Boyes we must get a look in the crater. He should be able to get some good picture from the thermal emission radiometer on board the Orion platform.

"Okay, doctor," Tom said. The *Seeker* is working on those images. What are you looking for?"

"I'm not sure but if my guess is right, I think I might know how they neutralized the effects of the XCFG gas and why we failed." Their conversation was interrupted by a voice on the radio.

"Nalowale base, this is *Seeker*. Do you copy?"

Jenson grabbed the microphone. "This is Nalowale, go ahead, *Seeker*."

"This is Commander Lee, we have some good closeup images of the center of that crater."

Walking to the radio Fleming motioned to Jenson to hand him the mike. "Commander, this is Dr. Fleming. Can you tell me what you see on the images?"

"Well, sir, I'm not sure, but it looks like there is a lot going on down there. From what I can tell it looks like a large concentration of these things in the center of the crater. One other thing, doc, our sensors are showing a signal of increasing intensity emanating from the same location. It's beginning to affect some of our systems.

I've never seen or heard anything like it."

"Commander, can you send us those images?"

"Yes, sir, we'll download them immediately."

"Fine, commander, I'll contact you as soon as I review the pictures."

"Understood, sir, we'll be standing by."

Replacing the microphone and turning to the group, Fleming said, "we have a lot to do and I fear not much time to do it."

"What are you talking about, doctor?" Jenson asked. "Don't you think you had better fill us in, and quickly?"

"Absolutely, Tom. I believe we made a serious miscalculation with the XCFG gas. We attacked the entire island instead of going after the main source."

As he spoke Deborah called out. "Doctor, we just received the images from the *Seeker*. I'll put them on the screen."

"Just as I suspected. You notice the heavy concentration of vegetation in the center of the crater that the commander spoke of?" he said, pointing to the screen. "This is their command center, so to speak. It is here that the strongest of the species have gathered and it is they that control and communicate with the others on Ahi, and below the sea. I believe the increased intensity of the signals that we have observed and that are even now affecting the *Seeker*, is a prelude to the next step in the evolution of this species. We must prevent that at all cost if we are to survive."

"That's swell, doc," Jenson said. "But unless I missed something, we're about out of options."

"I believe we have one more chance," Fleming replied. "But we're going to have to work fast and the timing must be precise."

"Well then, let's get on with it," Mike Ryan said running his hands through his hair.

"Agreed," said Fleming, and turning to Ryan he continued, "Mike, contact Captains Boyes and Fraser and ask them to meet me here. Tell them it is a matter of great urgency and I will explain everything when they arrive."

"Right, doc." Ryan answered and moved swiftly to the radio.

His attention now focused on Jenson, Fleming said, "Tom, that volcano is becoming very unstable and could endanger this island. We better move the villagers up to high ground. You know this island and these people so I want you to alert them immediately."

"I'll go with you," Deborah said, and together they headed for Keoniali's house. He and Keoni and the rest of the family were just finishing dinner when they walked in.

Deborah and Jenson looked at each other and started to laugh. They had completely lost track of the time.

"What's so funny?" Kuahiwi asked.

"I'm sorry, Kuahiwi; it's nerves and it's not funny," Jenson said "We came to warn you that Ahi could blow again and this could be a big one."

"I see," the older man said gravely.

"You've got to evacuate the village, and go to higher ground. If you start tonight, you can get them all out of here." He riffled through his pockets, and extracted some keyes. "Take my jeep. I'll help you alert the others."

As Tom and Deborah left Keoni's house the sky was already darkening. They moved quickly from house to house, explaining the danger and insisting that everyone leave immediately. Finally satisfied that Kuahiwi and his son could handle the rest, Jenson and Deborah returned to the house to see Boyes and Fraser enter ahead of them. As they themselves entered they saw Fleming usher the naval officers into the radio area.

Seeing them Fleming said, "Ah, good, we're all here. How is the evacuation proceeding?" he asked looking at Jenson.

"Everything is going smoothly."

"Good. Now gentlemen," he said looking at Boyes and Fraser. "I know that both of you have been fully briefed on all aspects of this incident, so I won't go over old ground. After reviewing the reports of the aircraft pilots and the data provided by the *Seeker* it is apparent that we face a far greater threat than we could have ever imagined. Our attempt to control this species with the cryogenic gas, though well intended, was sadly misdirected. It seems that the more dominant members of this species are gathered deep within that crater, probably spawned from the pods we placed there almost thirty years ago. Through their combined abilities they are controlling and directing the actions of all the other life forms on both islands.

"I believe our only remaining chance is to launch a two-pronged attack, which will require close coordination between your two vessels. If your assignments are not executed on schedule, we may very well face the possibility of an uninhabitable world."

Boyes and Fraser looked at each other, then back at Fleming. "Our orders say that you're in charge, doctor. Tell us what you need."

Fleming turned to Boyes and said, "Your job may be the most critical, captain. At exactly 0500 hours you will activate the HPM vircator and from your current submerged location you will direct a modulating pulse from 200 kilowatts to 30 GigaWatts towards Ahi Island.

"At the same time Captain Fraser, two of your aircraft must be over the volcano to release the remaining canisters of XCFG gas into the crater. This should trigger a twofold effect. The bombardment of the island with the modulating pulses will disrupt communication between the plants on the island and in the crater. The action of the gas should begin to destroy the controlling species in the crater. Hopefully, the combined effects of both will stop the evolution now taking place on the island and buy us some time. It's crucial, Captain Boyes, that you continue to transmit that pulse until the gas cloud is sufficiently developed. I don't believe this species will be able to defend itself and maintain control over the rest of the plants. Any questions, gentlemen?"

Fraser spoke up. "Yes, I have one."

"Yes captain?"

"What makes you think the gas will do the job this time when it had virtually no effect on the last run?"

"A fair question, captain. In our first attempt we tried to cover too large an area and to affect a large number of plants. The defensive heating process was more immediate because the density of the gas cloud was greatly reduced in the open air.

"This time we will concentrate on a tightly confined area containing a limited amount of the species. This should considerably increase the effectiveness of the gas."

"I hope you're right," Fraser said, as he and Boyes rose and prepared to depart.

"One last thing, gentlemen, by 0400 hours we must establish a secure communications link between this location, the *Seeker*, and the *Defiant*. It is imperative that we communicate during this operation."

"Good luck to all of us," Boyes said, and he and Fraser left the house.

-Fifteen-

At 0400 hours the communications link was established. The *Seeker* had submerged and taken a position one-half mile off Ahi Island. At 0430 hours two aircraft lifted off the deck of the *Defiant* and headed to the target area. Fleming and his team had stationed themselves at Jenson's house. The air was electrified with tension. As Fleming checked the computers that were monitoring the remote sensors on Ahi Island, the others waited anxiously, watching the clock tic off the minutes.

At 0500 hours the silence was broken. The *Seeker* reported that both it and the *Defiant* were in position and had begun their assault.

Dr. Fleming gazed into the small telescope and focused on Ahi Island. He scanned the lush tropical island surrounded by the blue water of the Pacific. "It's too bad we may have to destroy that Garden of Eden," he said to nobody in particular.

Evans snapped, "Better we destroy that garden than it destroy us."

"We all know what the doctor means, Ian," Deborah said. "He is doing what has to be done, so just take it easy."

Tom Jenson sat by the radio and watched the three of

them. Evans had shown his dislike for Fleming more than once and Deborah always flew to his defense. Jenson knew how Fleming felt, though. He himself had come to this island paradise never suspecting the hidden dangers, and now they were all fighting to save their culture from extinction, a danger brought about by the actions of men carelessly sowing the seeds of this new Eden.

Two long hours passed, they watched and listened in amazement as the strange life forms on Ahi challenged them for the right to survive. The intensity and power of the signals being transmitted was incredible. Sensors on board the *Seeker* and in the house were pushed far beyond the limits for which they had been designed.

Staring at the screen and shaking his head, Fleming muttered, "My God, what have we wrought."

"Look at this, Dr. Fleming," Deborah called out. "The seismic sensors indicate small tremors occurring across the island."

"Doctor," Jenson interrupted, "a message from the *Seeker*.

"What is it?" Fleming asked excitedly.

"They say something is happening in the volcano. They're not sure but it appears a pressure wave is forming, and there is some shifting of mass at the bottom of the crater."

"I was afraid of that," Fleming said pacing the floor. "I believe the pressure of the venting methane gas is affecting it. That combined with the interaction between the gas cloud and the heating effect produced by the botanical life may have caused that wave to develop. If it continues to build it could reactivate the volcano, and that would be devastating. I'm just thankful that we have moved the villagers to high ground.

"Tom, contact the *Seeker*. Tell Captain Boyes we believe the volcano may erupt very soon. Advise him to head out to open water and expect a tidal surge to follow the eruption, and have him contact the *Defiant* to do the same. Are aircraft from the *Defiant* still on station?"

"Yes, sir, they are."

"Ask them if they can see any sign of new fissures opening on the island."

Jenson contacted Iceman One and relayed Fleming's request. Turning back to Fleming, he said the pilot reported cracks opening up across the island.

"We better prepare for the worst," Fleming said. "I want to record as much of this event as possible. If we don't survive, hopefully somebody will know what happened here."

Suddenly, without warning, a deafening roar pierced the quiet island air. Violent flaming geysers of orange lava shot into the sky. The tremors began to increase and Nalowale started to shake. The huge new trees heavy with oversize fruit began to bend in the wind.

The conflict on Ahi intensified, and as they looked toward the volcano they could see the flaming orange lava spewing up and out over the sides of the crater.

Some of the villagers who had been hovering nearby began to panic. Jenson moved quickly to calm them while Deborah stared at the awesome sight in fascination. Then someone took her arm. It was Keoni's mother.

"Where is Keoni?" she cried. His father came up behind her and repeated the question.

"We'll find him," she assured them, dragging herself

away from the spectacle. Suddenly Jenson was beside her.

"Where's Keoni?" he too asked.

"That's what we'd all like to know. I'm going to look for him."

"No!" he shouted. "It's too dangerous. Go back to the house. I'll take the jeep and see if I can find him." He grabbed her arm, but she wrenched away. "Not without me!"

"All right, get in. There's no time to argue."

But after twenty minutes they both knew it was hopeless. The ground beneath them had begun to shake, and they turned back to the house, dodging falling trees and debris that flew by them, driven by the wind.

There, standing in the doorway of Tom's house, was Keoni.

"Where've you been?" he shouted.

All at once the tension faded, and Deborah grabbed him and hugged him and cried. Jenson ran ahead to Mike Ryan and the others in the radio room, partly to get the news and partly so that she could not see his own tears.

"Iceman One," a voice crackled from the radio.

"Come in, Iceman One," Ryan said.

"We're pulling out of here, Nalowale. That mountain looks ready to break apart."

"How bad is it, Iceman One?"

"The whole island's covered with ash and black smoke. It looks like it's breaking apart. I have to sign off. The heat is intensifying and my compass is useless. Iceman One out."

"Roger, Iceman One, God speed," Ryan said

releasing the microphone

Deborah moved over to the sensor panels. The signals from Ahi had intensified.

"How long can they last, Dr. Fleming?" Ryan asked. "They seem to be on the attack now."

"Possibly," Fleming replied. "But I don't think so. I think they know they're locked in a life-and-death struggle."

"Come here," Evans yelled, "and take a look at the beach." They followed him back outside. The air was filled with a strange hissing sound and the blue Pacific was churning in an angry rage. As they watched, the sea suddenly withdrew to the coral reef thirty feet from shore, leaving a vast expanse of beach suddenly exposed and littered with fish gasping for air.

"It's beginning," Jenson whispered, "the tidal surge is just beginning."

They stood there, transfixed, as the water began to rise and swell up at the edge of the reef. It grew higher and higher until it was about thirty feet in the air, then suddenly reversed direction back toward the island at about twenty miles per hour.

Running back to the house, they secured all the windows and huddled on the floor of the radio room. A great wall of water crashed down on the tiny island, smashing windows, sweeping furniture and household articles along in its path; houses collapsed like children's toys and others were swept whole from their foundation and carried several yards away.

A series of three giant waves pounded the island, each one bigger and more powerful, building into a crescendo until the final wave, close to one hundred feet, seemed to cover the entire island, moving huge coral boulders and spilling them everywhere.

For two hours nature vented her anger. The islanders huddled together like shipwrecked survivors as the waves pounded around the island. Then suddenly the waters withdrew for the last time and the tidal surge was over as quickly as it had begun.

Shaken but thankful to have survived, they stood up and walked cautiously to the lanai. A huge black cloud now hung over the water and everything was quiet and still where the huge volcano had been

"It's gone," Deborah said looking toward Ahi Island. "The entire island is gone."

Evans was back at the seismograph. "There's nothing there, Dr. Fleming. The whole damned island sank."

"It appears that nature has solved a problem we could not," Fleming said dryly.

"This is strange," said Jenson approaching the others. "I just received a message from the *Seeker*. They say their sensors picked up a powerful signal during the last few minutes before the island disappeared."

"What's so strange about that?" asked Evans. "Those thing were sending signals continually."

"Well, it seems that this signal was sent straight up. A call for help maybe? They say that it was powerful enough to reach deep into space, well beyond our solar system."

"Are they sure?" injected Fleming, in an unsettling voice.

"Yes, sir," replied Jenson. "They tracked it for over five minutes.

"Well, it's over now," Deborah said, walking to the

large window and gazing out towards the bubbling water that once was Ahi Island.

"Let's say it's finished for the time being," Fleming mused. "Let's hope that if it should happen again we'll be better prepared to deal with it."

"Yes, doctor," Jenson agreed. "But you know, as glad as I am to see this thing finished, I can't help thinking."

"Thinking about what?" Mike asked.

"What we might have learned if we could have communicated with them instead of confronting them."

"We may never know, Tom," Fleming replied. "The distressing fact is that they were everywhere. We just didn't care till they made us notice them."

"Boy, it sure has been one hell of an experience," Ryan said, shaking his head. "I hope we never have to go through that again. Like the doc says, nature had to correct its own mistake."

"Mistake, Mike?" Fleming cautioned. "I wonder."

"What do you mean?"

"I wonder, was it a mistake or a test? We faced the unforeseen and this time we survived. But I have a strange feeling there will be a next time. . . ."

-Epilogue-

Roberta Stone of Charlottesville, Virginia, tended to the plants in her green house as she regularly did. An active member of the local Garden Club, she particularly sought out exotic plants. She was very excited with the odd new plants she had brought back from her recent trip to the Hawaiian Islands. The cuttings were doing so well that they began to take over the entire greenhouse. To their delight, she had brought back enough to give cuttings to each member of the club. They were all as fascinated as she was with the odd triangular leaves and the resilience of the plants. They seemed to thrive everywhere.

She settled into the white wicker rocker. Normally she listened to classical music, as she rested. She said it was very pleasing to her plants and was sure that she could see them swaying gently while it played. But lately the annoying interference made that impossible. No one could explain it. Maybe it was solar activity, since it was affecting the entire area.

She yawned and cooled herself by the fan. Lately, she had felt so tired she could hardly get through the day. She gazed proudly at her prize collection of flourishing green plants. She leaned back and closed her eyes as an eerie mist slowly settled around her.

Early in September, Sven Olson and his fiancé drove up to Washington State for a long awaited camping trip in the great pine forest. After unpacking their equipment they made supper over an open fire and gazed around at the spectacular view. The trees seemed greener and taller than any he had remembered. Sitting back in their folding chairs they pulled a wool blanket over their legs.

They became drowsy; it must have been the long drive, Sven thought. Suddenly they were very tired. They placed the blanket on the ground and lay down on the lush pine-covered earth of the forest. The crackling fire began to die, but they did not notice as they both fell into an eternal sleep.

Far to the south, Tony Cummings was celebrating the end of summer vacation by diving off Catalina Island. His blond hair was bleached almost white and his muscular body was evenly tanned from his leisure hours in the sun.

He sat on his rented boat and headed out to sea. His bronzed skin glistened with salt water and his wet blond hair clung to his face and neck. Two miles out he turned the engine off and put on his wet suit, checked his air tank and facemask, and then slipped backwards into the beautiful clear water. Slowly he dove deeper and enjoyed the fantastic view of marine life and vegetation. The red abalone along the sea bottom was a treasure for fishermen.

He glided through the water snapping pictures of the aquatic wonderland around him. Not even Neptune relished the beauty of the sea more, he thought as he swam among the rock formations and then headed for the surface.

Exhilarated by the experience, he stood on the deck and rechecked his air gauge and decided to make a final dive. Replacing his facemask he again rolled backwards into the water not noticing the strange mass of kelp floating nearby.

He was about twenty feet down when his foot was entangled in a tentacle-like object. Removing his knife he cut himself free and, making his way to the surface, he reached for the small ladder on the side of the boat. As he put his hand on the first rung the object again ensnared his foot. But as he struggled to break free, a second tentacle struck his face and body. He tried to scream but no sound was heard.

Startled, he released his grip on the ladder to protect his face. Tony was griped with fear as he felt himself being pulled beneath the sea. Something cold and wet was holding him down. He struggled with all his might to pull free, but he only became more entangled. Now he was totally ensnared in the huge mass of green plant tentacles, and as it enveloped his body, and he struggled to breathe, he gulped salty seawater. Filled with disbelief he sank below the sea.

Three days later his body washed ashore, a bewildered look still on his face and clutched in his hand a small piece of seaweed that moved unnoticed.

Early in January 2008, the space shuttle *Explorer*, the newest of the shuttle fleet, was preparing to begin the check off procedures for reentry, having successfully completed one of the most uniquely different missions in the program's long history.

The crew had spent the past ten days conducting tests

on the effects of weightlessness, zero gravity, and the ability, from six hundred miles in space, to communicate and respond to specific events occurring at mission control, as they circled the earth at 17,300 mph.

What had generated the interest and excitement for this mission was that, for the first time, the subjects were not human but botanical in nature.

The mission's purpose was to provide answers to ongoing questions raised in the early sixties, about the remarkable ability demonstrated by the life form we call plants, and to determine to what extent their abilities affected our very existence.

They had been testing a hybrid species of plant found on the remote Pacific island that had resulted from a bizarre incident, which still sent chills through those who had been involved and knew the terrifying story.

"Control, this is *Explorer*. We are at landing minus two hours, beginning descent checklist, over."

"Roger, *Explorer*, this is Control. Confirm landing at minus two hours starting descent checklist, Control out"

The crew had just unstowed the seats for the mission, and payload specialists, all had assumed landing positions when they saw it approaching.

"What the hell is that?" asked flight commander Colonel William (Buck) Welsh, as he looked out the cockpit window.

"I don't know," replied Major Meg Collins, the shuttle pilot, as she looked in the direction he was pointing. "I've never seen anything like it before."

"Well, whatever it is, it's coming right at us," said Welsh, as he continued to watch the object

"Control, this is Explorer. You guys tracking anything

up our way? Over."

"Explorer, this is Control. That's negative. Is there a problem? Over."

"Control, this is Explorer. Not yet, but we've got company up here. Over."

"Explorer, repeat. Did you say company? Over."

"That is affirmative, Control. We have an unidentified object now stationary in close proximity to our craft. We are getting some pictures. You guys will really have something to look at when we get back. Over."

"Explorer, this is Control. We copy. Are you in any trouble? Over."

"Not yet, Control. Whatever it is, it's just sitting out there looking us over. Wait a minute. What's that-----?" All faces at Houston Control turned toward the display screen as they strained to hear something from the Explorer. For a heart- pounding ten seconds, there was silence.

Then they cheered as they heard the unmistakable drawl of Colonel Buck Welsh.

"Control, this is Explorer. Do you copy? Over."

"We read you loud and clear, Explorer. What the hell happened? Is everyone okay up there? Over."

"That's affirmative, Control. It appears we were hit with some type of probe. All the systems went down for a few seconds, but everything looks okay now. We're running a diagnostic check to be sure. Over."

"Explorer, this is Control. Do you still have visual contact with the unknown? We have had negative radar contact with the object. Over."

"That's negative, Control, We've lost contact with the object. According to our computers, the light beam that hit us scanned all the ship's systems. Everything is on line now, and we are reinitializing descent procedures at landing minus one hour fifty minutes. Over."

"Roger, reinitializing landing at one hour fifty minutes. Keep your eyes open up there just in case our visitor is still in the area. Over."

"Control, this is Explorer. Roger, we'll call you in about twenty minutes. Over."

"Roger, Explorer. Control out."

During the next twenty minutes, the shuttle crew prepared for deorbit. They first checked the Orbital Maneuvering System (OMS) engine status; then the Reaction Control System (RCS); then initiated prestart of the Auxiliary Power Unit (APU). With these checks completed, they again contacted Mission Control.

"Control, this is Explorer. APU prestart complete. Over."

"Roger, Explorer. Control, out."

They loaded the deorbit computer program and entered the start code. Now at landing minus one hour and fifteen minutes, they waited for the go or no-go decision to begin deorbit entry

"Explorer, this is Control. You are 'GO' for deorbit burn."

"Roger, Control. Go for deorbit burn. Explorer, out."

Major Collins maneuvered the shuttle into burn attitude, turning it around until it was flying tail first. Confirming single APU restart with Houston Control, she armed the OMS engines.

"Control, this is Explorer. OMS engines are armed. Over."

"Roger, Explorer. Copy OMS armed. Control out."

With the firing of its engines, the shuttle began its controlled descent. At an altitude of 400,000 feet and thirty minutes until touch down, they reentered the earth's atmosphere at 17,000 mph.

"Control, this is Explorer. We are at entry interface. Stand by for loss of signal."

"Roger, Explorer. Control, out."

As the shuttle passed through the ionized particles of the atmosphere's upper layer, radio communications were lost. Once clear of the blackout area the shuttle again contacted Houston control.

"Control, this is Explorer. Do you copy? Over."

"We copy, Explorer. You're looking good. Over."

After completing its final maneuvers the shuttle safely landed at the Kennedy Space Center, as a strange object plummeted unnoticed into the waters off the Florida coast, and quietly settled to the bottom.

On January 31, 2008 NASA's long range ORION satellite detected an unusual signal interfering with global communications. The signal seemed to originate from Epsilon Eridani, a distant star in the Constellation Eridanus, located a mere 10 light-years from earth.

Printed in the United States
3659

9 781931 633420